Praise for *Quest & The Sign*

"A symbiosis of words and images ʋʜɑʋ propels the reader on a breathless ride into the realms of spirit, wonder, and terror. The words are sharp, the images sublime, the experience unique. This is a book not to be missed."
Ian Whates - Author of *Pelquin's Comet*

"Cockshaw's visually haunting images perfectly suit Malan's enthralling storytelling."
Jay Johnstone - Tolkien Artist

"Epic and haunting. Viscerally realised in a shadowy dream-time, where warrior courage and philosophical questioning are needed to open the way."
Ricardo Pinto - Author of *The Stone Dance of the Chameleon* trilogy

"The images impacted on me first. As an artist, that's where my eye was inevitably drawn. A dark journey indeed, through a strange, disturbing abstraction of powerful photographic and digital visuals. I haven't encountered anything quite like it before.
But then, engaging with the written story in the first half, and the more demanding poetic concrete of the second half … it is a symbiosis of words and images that takes one on a darkly epic and nightmare voyage.
A quite extraordinary feat of the imagination."
Jim Burns - SF & Fantasy Artist

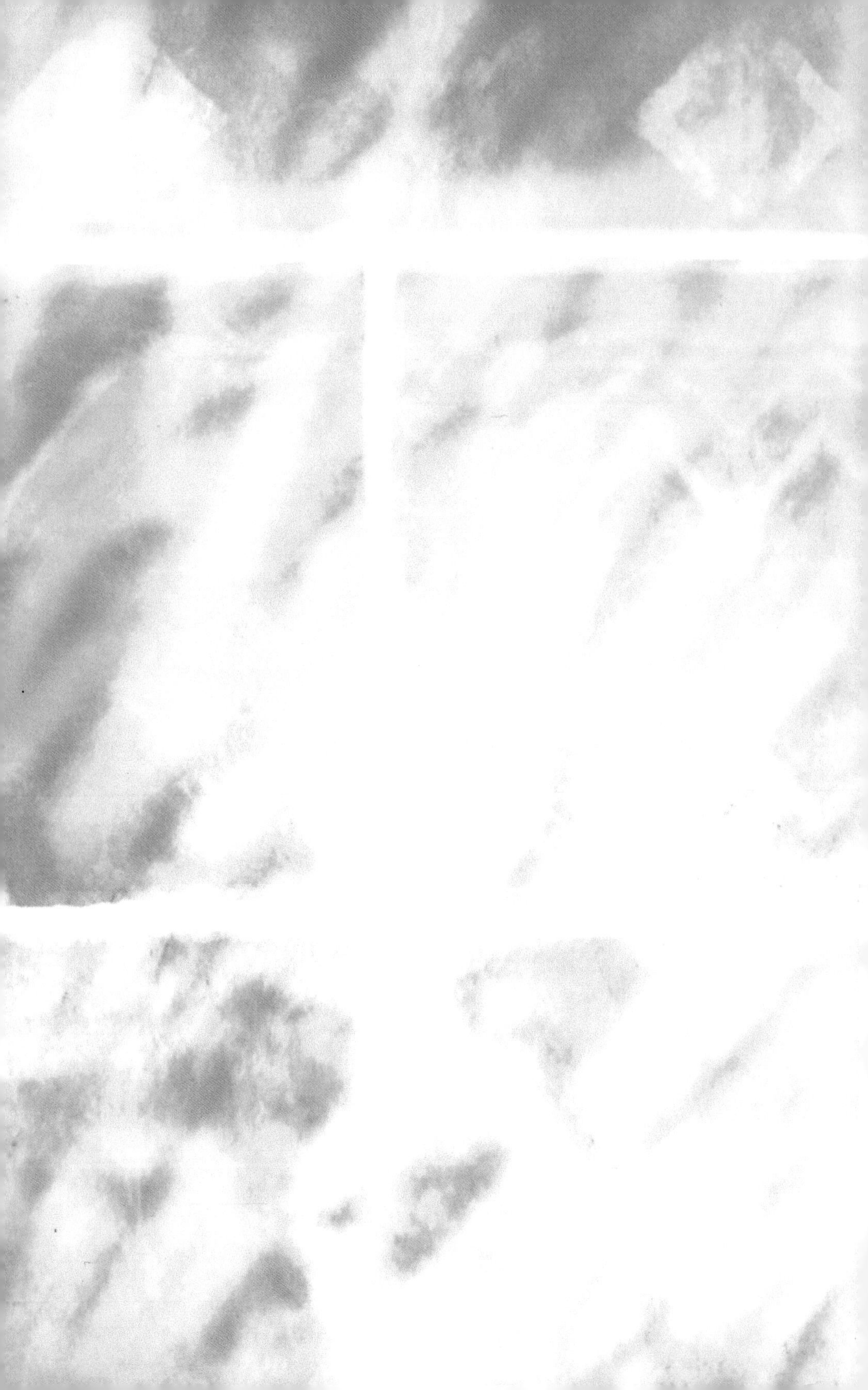

A DARKNESS IN MIND

QUEST
&
THE SIGN OF
THE SHINING BEAST

WRITTEN BY
ROBERT S MALAN

ILLUSTRATED BY
JOHN COCKSHAW

First Published 2016 by Luna Press Publishing

'A Darkness In Mind' Concept, Quest and Text Copyright © Robert S Malan 2015
'The Sign of the Shining Beast' Concept and Images Copyright © John Cockshaw 2015
'A Darkness In Mind' Logo Design John Cockshaw
Book Design by Francesca T Barbini

ISBN: 978-1-911143-01-7

WWW.LUNAPRESSPUBLISHING.COM

For James and Andrew,
my brothers, critics, co-conspirators
and superb men of books, art,
science and mischief.

John

For my family: Mom, Dad, Dave
& Sharon. May the Way always be
lit for you.
  Most of all, to Francesca, the
driving force (an almighty force)
behind all that is good in my life.
  ... and Monkey to Mountain,
where it all began.

Robert

To Jo
Peace & light on the
path. Be a warrior.

Akecheta

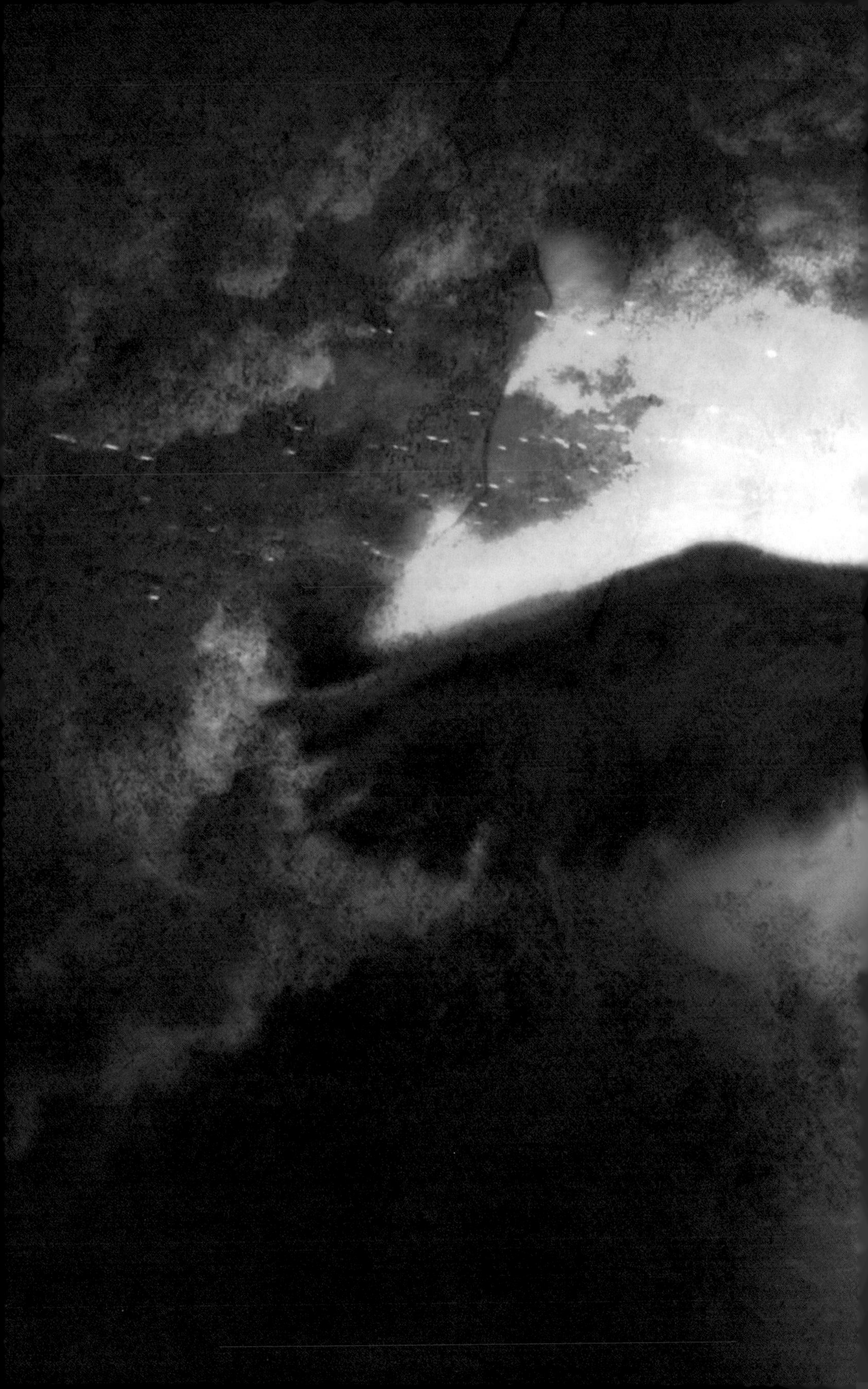

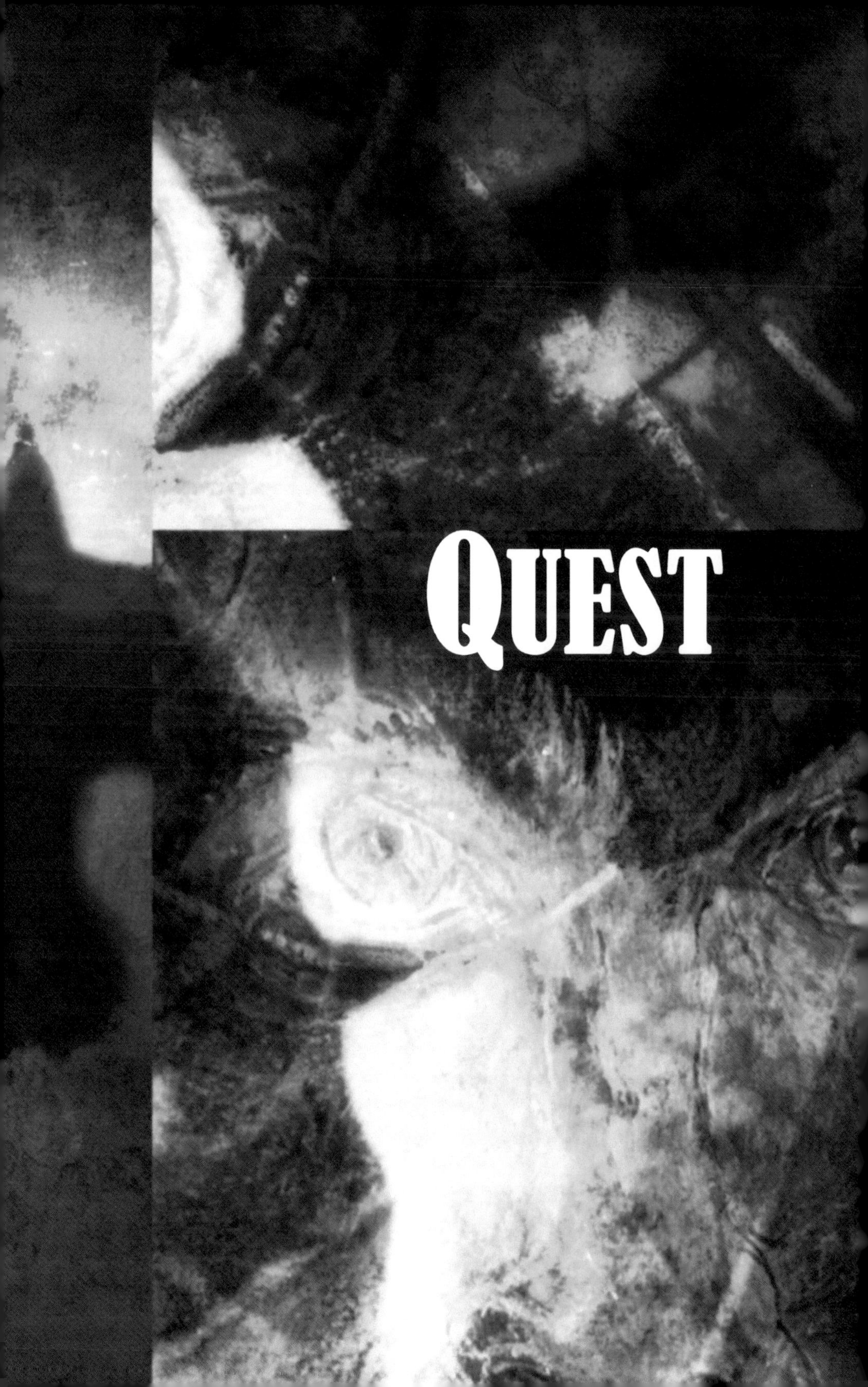
QUEST

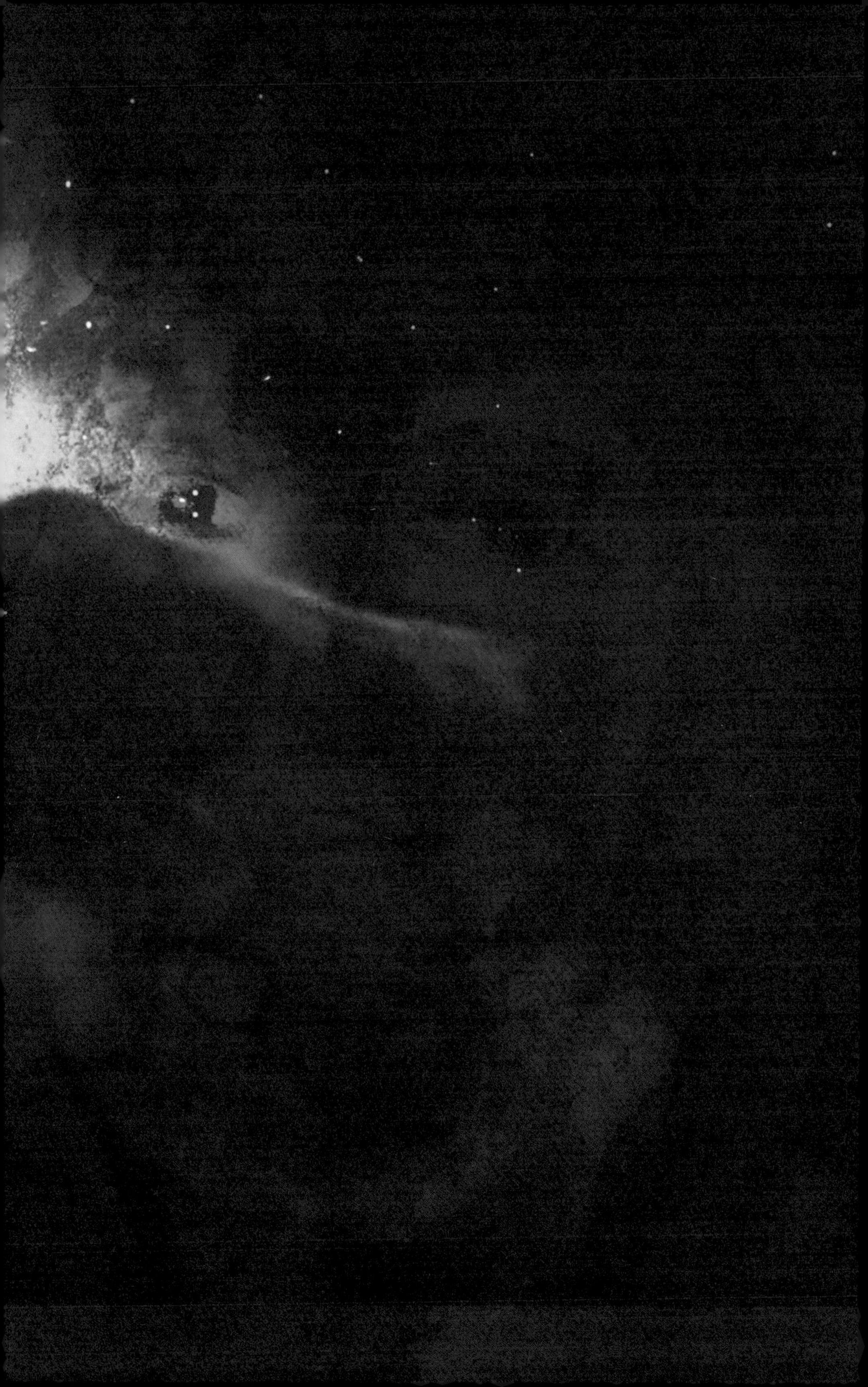

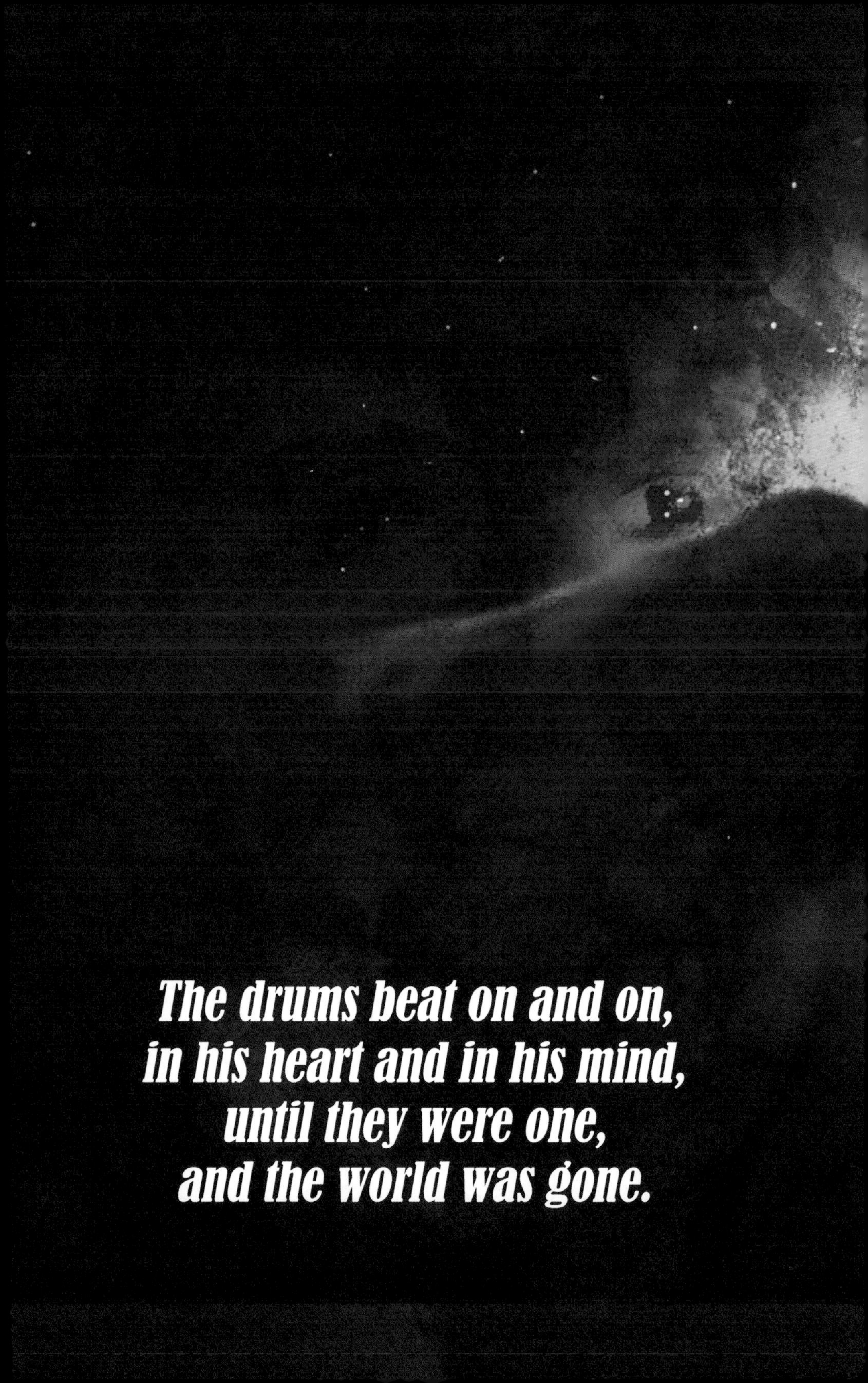
The drums beat on and on,
in his heart and in his mind,
until they were one,
and the world was gone.

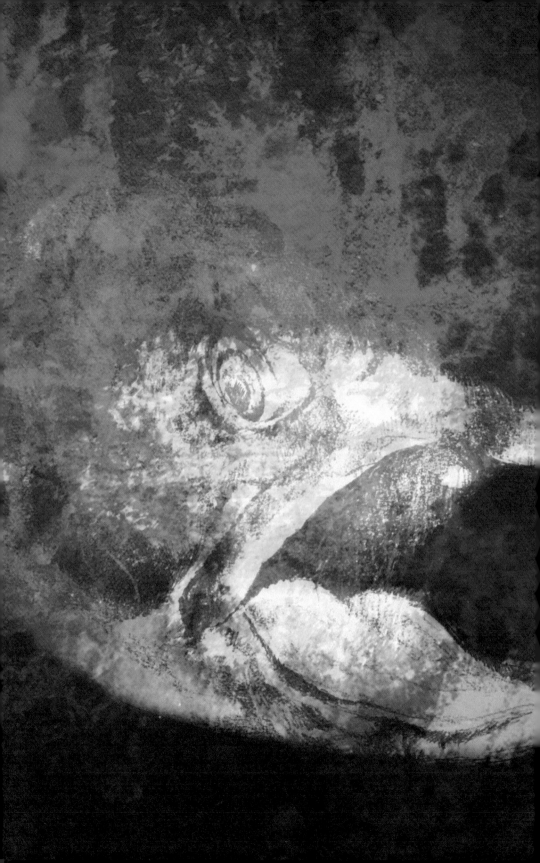

(The Pale)

Darkness. Complete. Overwhelming.

Was this how it had always been, in the time ...

... *before* ...

... *after?*

The darkness wasn't empty. It had substance - thick and cloying; murky liquid. It closed in on him as he woke.

Breathe! his mind screamed at him.

'*Not yet!*' Another voice commanded. '*Up, now. Swim.*'

He held his breath and kicked upward. Distant light shimmered into view and he swam frantically toward it. An instant later, he broke the surface, gasping. Air streamed into his lungs.

He blinked, treading water. All around was a giant spherical cavern; at its edges, a rocky ledge encircled the pool. Along it, bloated crimson worms gnawed at earthen walls. High above, an opening yawned, letting in a single shaft of sun.

'*Below. Danger!*' That strange, compelling voice again.

The water under his feet shifted, almost imperceptibly, but it was enough. He dipped his head back under and saw a dark mass rising toward him. A huge, fleshy mouth gaped open. Instinct kicked in. He grabbed the top of the mouth as it reached for him, and pushed his feet down against it. The bottom lip slapped shut as the creature leapt from the water, forcing him out with it.

It was in full view now: a giant fish, its oily skin a sickly grey. The fish snapped its head, flipping him clear and its mouth gawped open once more. He somersaulted, riding the motion of the throw so he was facing straight down as he fell toward it.

The fish snapped hungrily at him, even as it too began to plummet, but his arc was perfectly aimed. He landed just above its mouth, between its eyes, and punched at the right one. The fish thrashed in silent agony.

They splashed down into the pool. Water gushed up and over him, threatening to overwhelm him with its suffocating grasp. He fought through the surging foam and kicked clear. As the fish dove away, down into the gloom, he surfaced and swam for the ledge at the edge of the pool.

When he reached water's edge, he pulled himself up and collapsed there on his back, allowing himself a moment of rest. The strange worms burrowed into the walls, oblivious of him. He watched them, suddenly hypnotised by the slow rhythmic squirming of their bodies and the faint rustle of their chewing.

But now he saw, it wasn't soil they were burrowing into at all; there was no mistaking that the texture was changing before his eyes. The gnawing became a sickening squelch as the worms ploughed deeper into it. And then there was the smell; it struck him in a wave, forcing its way up his nostrils and smothering his senses: a nauseating, rotting stench. It was as if the cavern were the innards of a giant, bloated carcass. Horrified, he scrambled to his feet.

Still the sound of the gnawing worms grew louder, until it was a cacophony; biting, ceaseless devouring. And he knew then that they would consume him too if he stayed there.

I have to get out!

He scanned the surface of the water before him.

Black, so black.

Unbroken.

An endless expanse.

The cold heart of existence.

What is this? I can't ... Is this how it was before ...

... after?

All he could see now was the darkness, unending. The ground beneath his feet was gone. There was no way out, no escape. Here he stood, in nothingness, suspended. He was suddenly beyond, in a place where sound and light were non-existent. A realisation, something half-remembered and fleeting, sprung into focus and was gone just as quickly.

A single large fish plopped suddenly into view in the distance. Then another. And another. They were dead, their eyes flat and unseeing. He was back again, the cavern all around him; the fishes floating on their sides in the dark pool; the worms squirming, burrowing behind him. And still more fishes popped to the surface, until they were covering the surface of the pool. Soon so many were appearing that they were pushing the ones at the centre of the pool up, forming a mound that began to overflow and slide towards the outer edges.

The Voice filled his mind: '*Get out! Death here.*'

How? I ... I don't know the way.

No reply. If he stayed where he was, it was clear he would be consumed, drowned in a flood of dead fish or eaten by the worms. So he scrambled for the only route he could see, across the growing pile of carcasses. Still it expanded, ever upwards. He faltered, feet floundering on the ghastly, slippery surface. But just as he felt himself sliding, beyond recovery, he

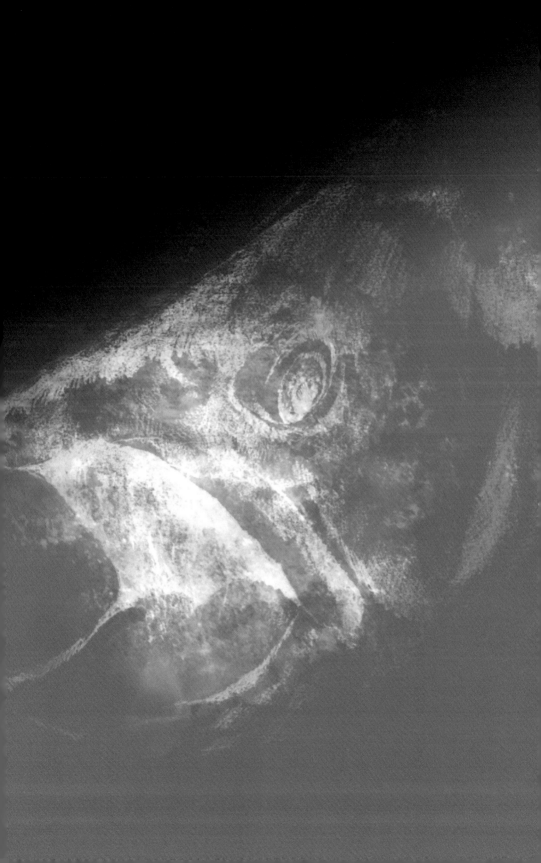

saw a vision, of a grey and white fish sailing, leaping up a stream, even as the waters slapped at it, forcing it backwards. It did not falter.

He forced himself forward, and leapt for the opening; it was near, so near. His hands met the soil at the edge of the opening and his fingers sunk deep into it, like they had suddenly become worms, burrowing into earth. He hung there for a moment, and then clambered up.

There was no looking back - below lay only death.

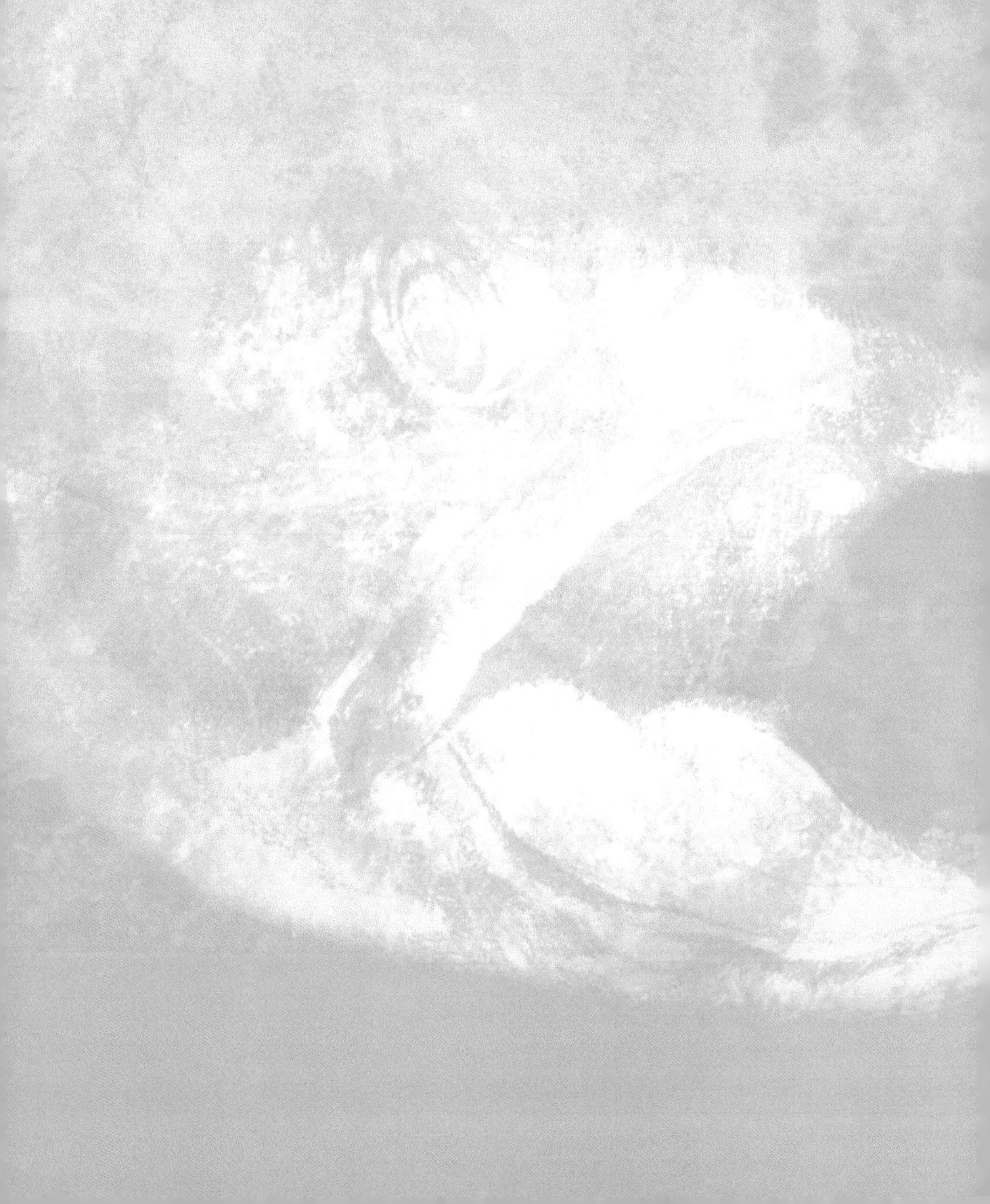

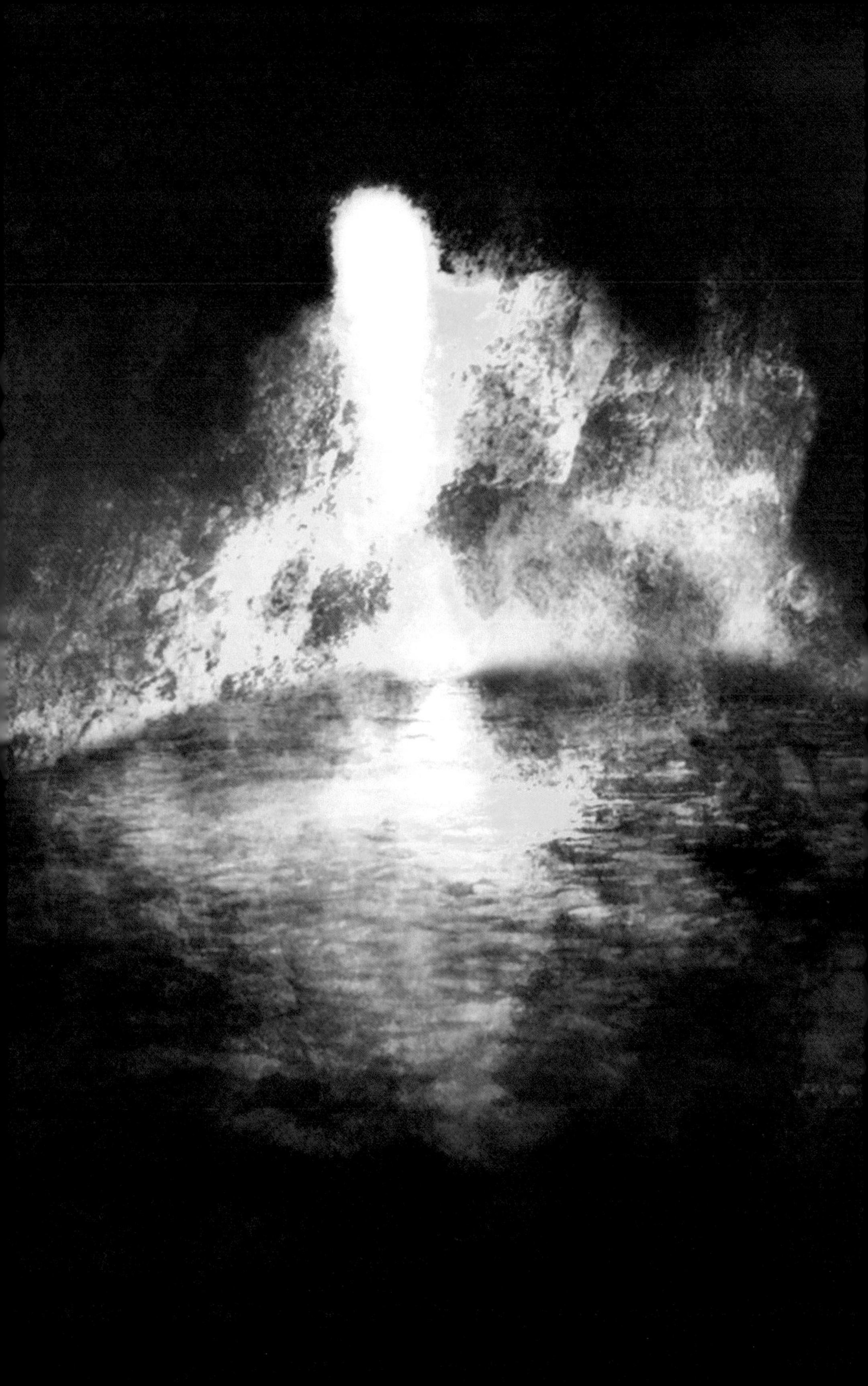

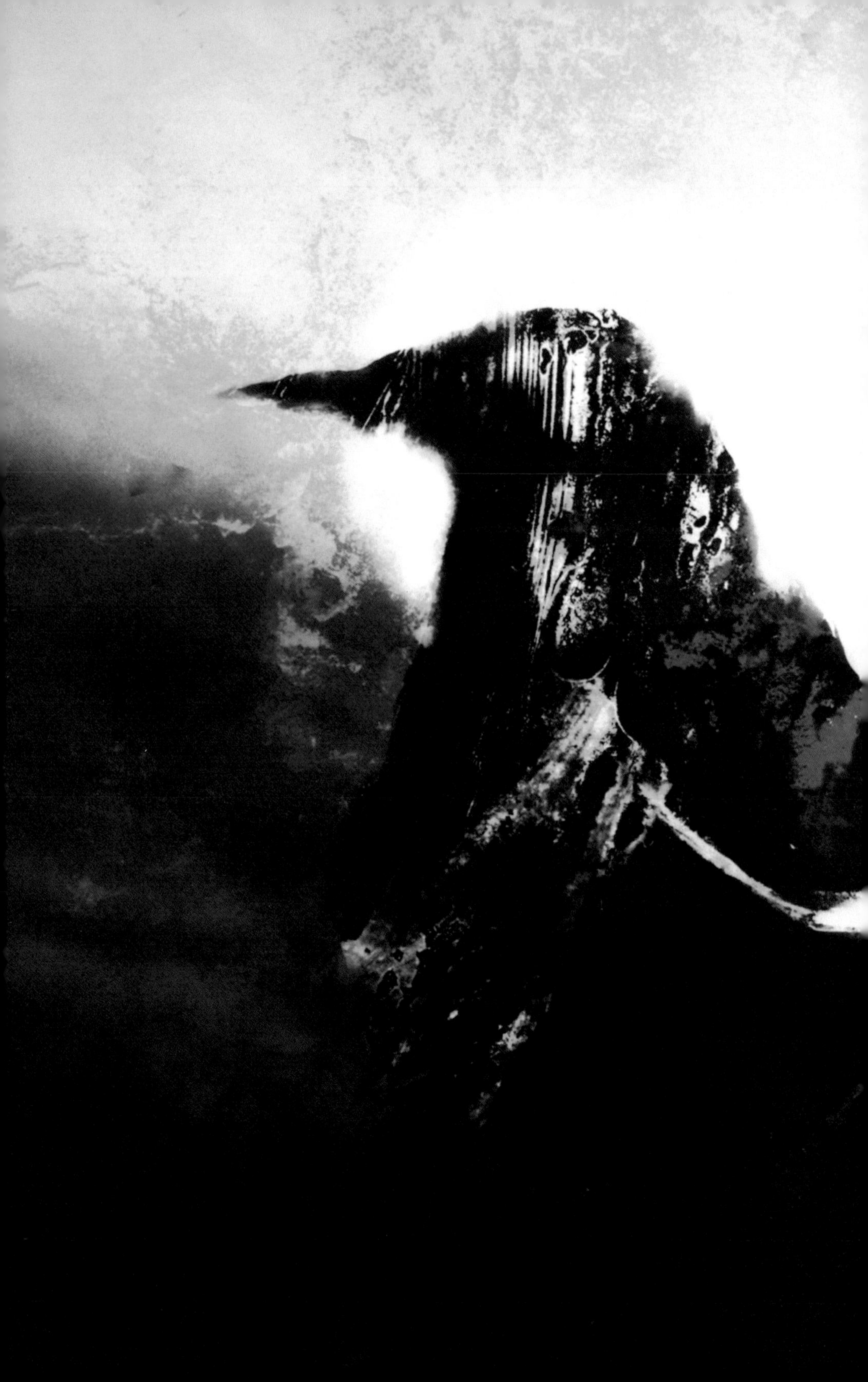

(Light)

Bright sunshine greeted him on the other side of the opening. He blinked, adjusting to the glare. In the midst of a vast, open field he stood. Lush green blades of grass rose up to chest-height as far as the eye could see. He wondered if something was wrong with his perspective, because it didn't seem right for the grass to be that length. As he studied his surroundings, he realised it was not that it was too long - he was smaller. It instantly disorientated him as the comprehension of this hit home.

'*Clear your mind - it is different here. Find the way.*' The Voice again.

He scouted the horizon, searching. 'Where are you? I can't remember-' he called out.

'*Wait. The path is opening.*'

He scanned the clear blue sky, which was unbroken, save for a few wisps of cloud. His eyes were drawn to a speck in the distance, growing larger, taking shape as it drew nearer. Soon he was able to make out two blurred lines to either side of it.

Raven.

The ground beneath him rumbled and he turned to look at the opening he had emerged from, half expecting to see a dead fish pop through it. Instead, dark, black ooze seeped over the verge, spreading along the ground towards him.

He ran from it.

'*Wait!*' the Voice urged.

'I can't. Not here. I can't let it-'

But then he did halt, frozen in his tracks, because he suddenly saw how close the raven was, its jet-black beak pointed threateningly at him as it slowed and then swooped. Instinct kicked in once more and a strange calm fell over him, guided by some deeper knowledge. He fell onto his back, curling himself into a ball. Sharp talons clutched at him; he didn't recoil from them but instead shot his legs up to meet them. In his mind, he saw his feet becoming talons themselves; instantly, they transformed, and gripped the raven's claws.

It shrieked and yanked away. Wings beat furiously against his sides. He held tight and forced his upper body up to meet it, clutching hold of two feathery handfuls, then threw himself over its nape and swung his legs around its neck. The raven's cawing grew frantic and it floundered, desperate to free itself of this unexpected counterattack.

A strange calm descended on him, despite the bucking of the bird. He could sense its movements before they happened, as if it had become a part of him, or *he* of *it*. He eased his grip and caressed the skin beneath its plumage. '*Easy, brother bird. Fly! You know the way.*'

And like that, it stopped. The raven's desperate flapping eased and steadied, until it was flying serenely over the ground. The mad struggle of before seemed another lifetime ago. Now, in this moment, they were one. The bird veered to the side and shot away.

He relaxed and closed his eyes. Cool air streaked against his cheeks as his mind turned to thoughts of things half-remembered, half-forgotten, but never gone. He thought of earth and sky and moon and stream and ...

... *starving, thirsty, weeping children, their hands held up to him, pleading* ...

His eyes shot open, and he shook his head, disturbed by the image, not sure what to make of it. Although his heart was suddenly heavy, he had to ignore it and push on. Time was short; he knew this - not why or how - but he knew it nonetheless, somewhere beneath the fog that lay over large parts of his memory.

You must find the way.

He looked once more to the horizon. Up ahead was a vast tree, cradling boughs like the arms of giants, melded onto a great, unflinching oaken body. Upon the boughs lay clusters of emerald leaves.

He opened his mouth to say something to the bird, but no words he recognised emerged. Instead, a stream of melodic sound gushed forth from him; a singsong language he didn't fully comprehend, but somehow understood, deep in the recesses of his mind. The bird seemed to understand too, for it slowed and drew close to the foot of the tree.

He leapt to the ground, raised his head and scanned the tree. The grooves within its bark meandered in a hypnotic pattern along its exterior, up to its branches, and the leafy, verdure ceiling high above him.

He turned then and looked back at the raven. It had landed and stood there, regarding him. Unbidden, as if driven by an invisible force, he lifted his right arm, palm open, to the bird. As he did this, his hand tingled and grew warm. He retracted it and examined the skin; etched against his palm was the dark outline of a bird, wings spread wide. His eyes drifted up again to the raven and he saw that it was poised, mirroring the outline on his hand. Then it dipped its head once, cawed and flew off. He watched as it disappeared into the distance, suddenly sad but not knowing why.

'*Wakanda* - with you goes my soul,' he whispered.

As the words left his lips, he felt suddenly numb, his feet rooted to the floor. While he watched, a wave of darkness swept up over the horizon and blotted out the sun. The sound of the gnawing worms filled his head

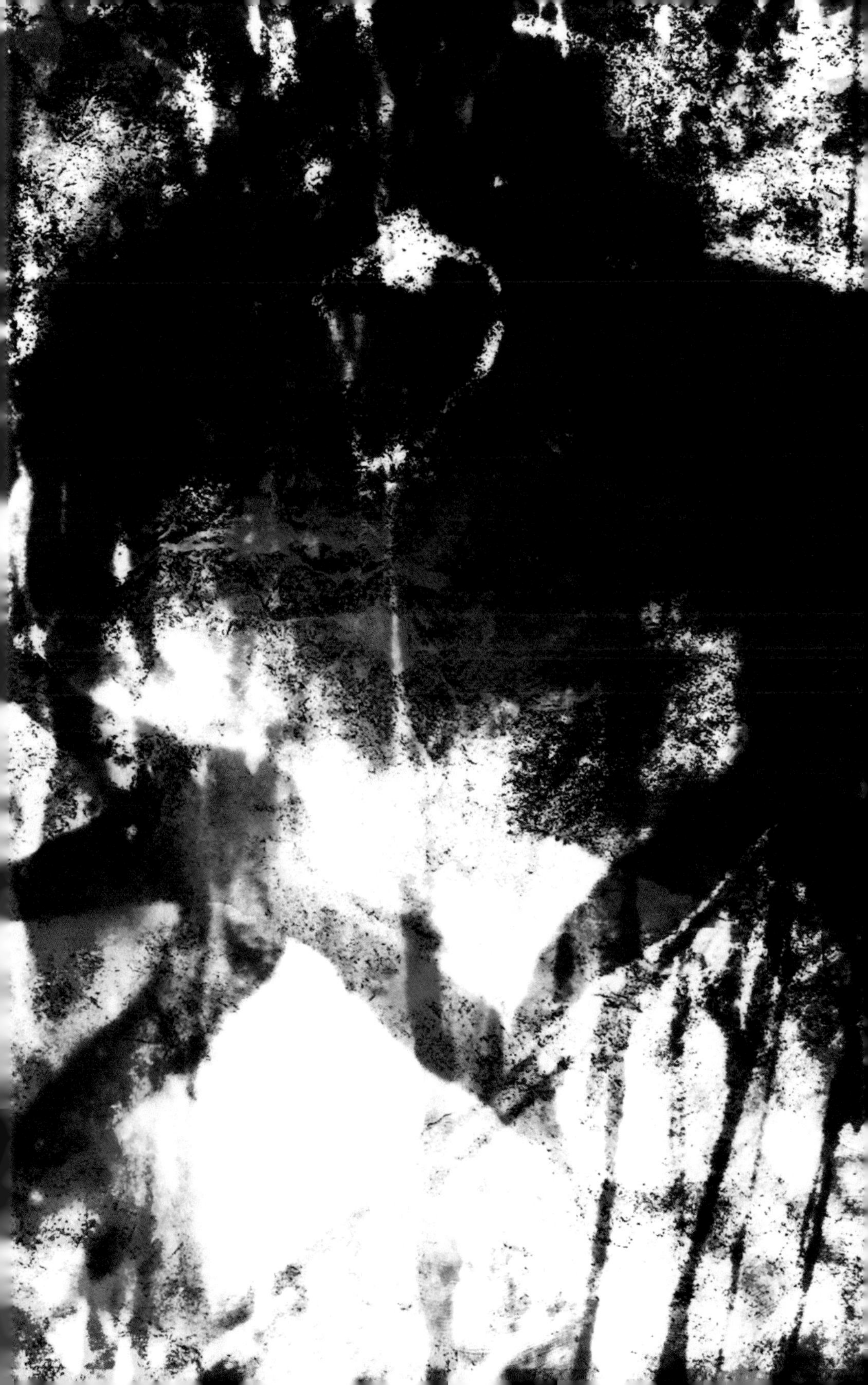

again. He stood, petrified, transfixed.

'*Go!*' the Voice screamed to him. '*The tree!*'

It was as if all will had drained from him, sucked up into the inexorable darkness that was advancing on him. But he forced himself to move, or at least something did. He turned and sprinted to the base of the tree, throwing his hands against its surface as he reached it. At once, a large, square door appeared and opened silently inwards. He hurried through and it slipped shut behind him.

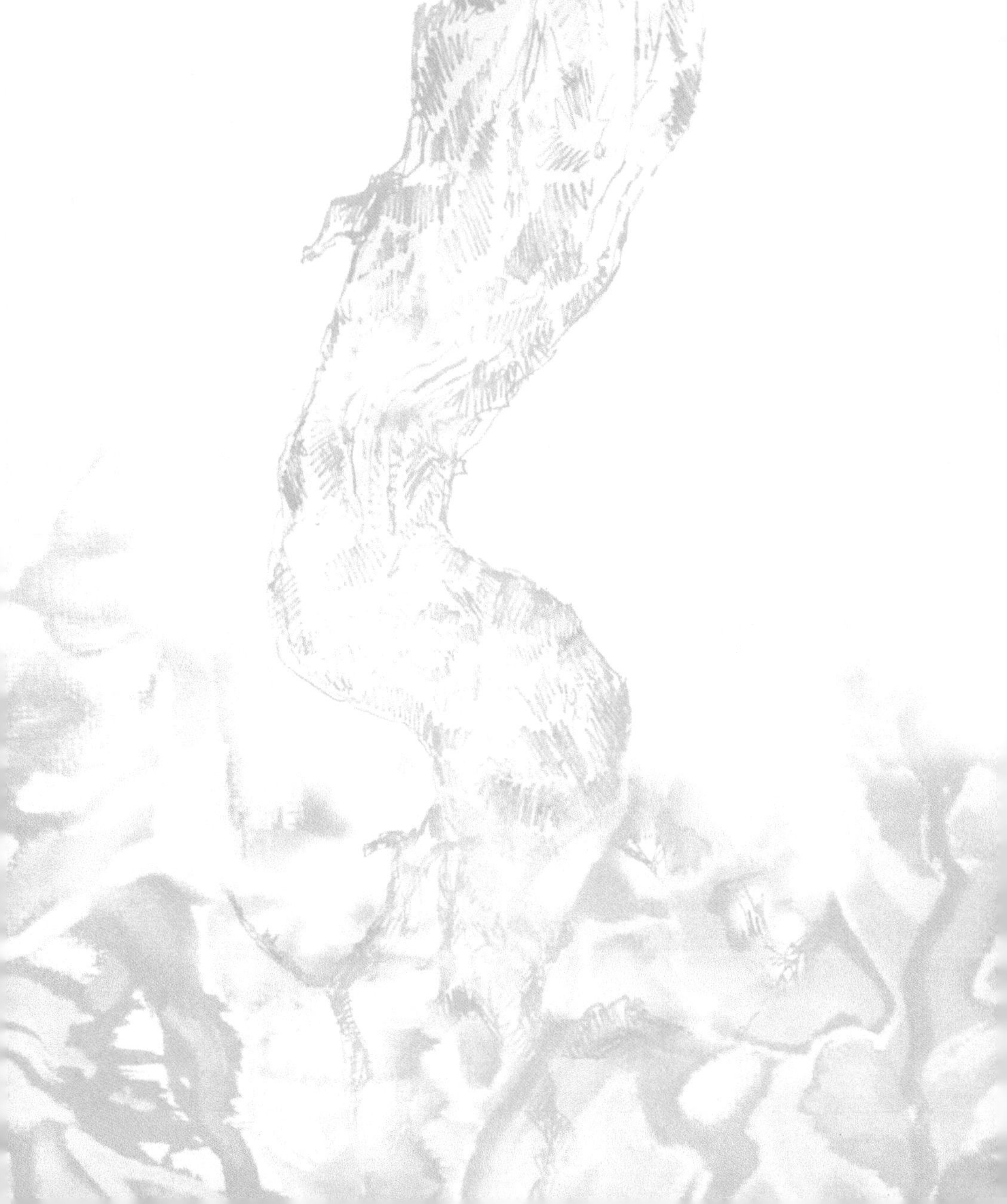

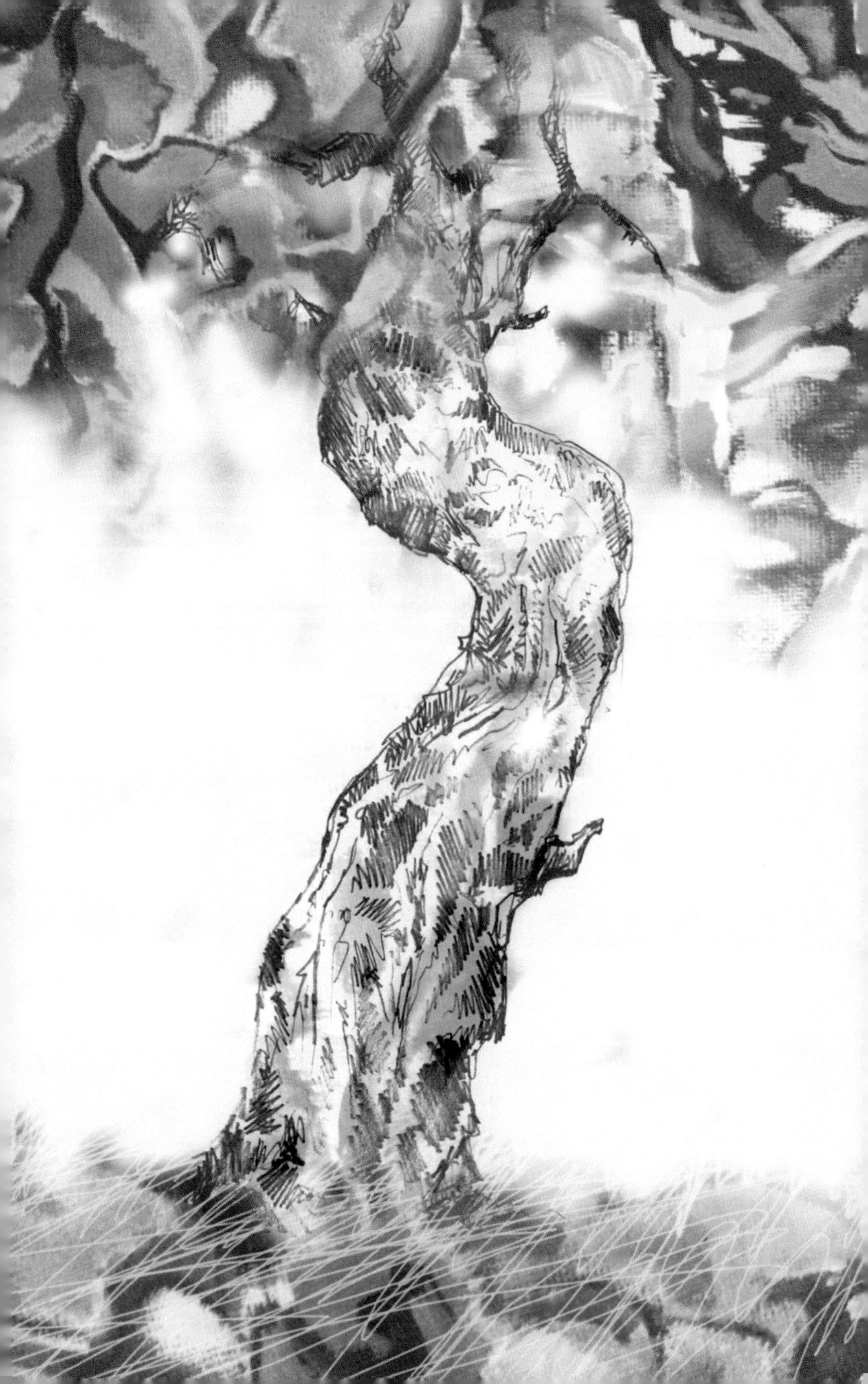

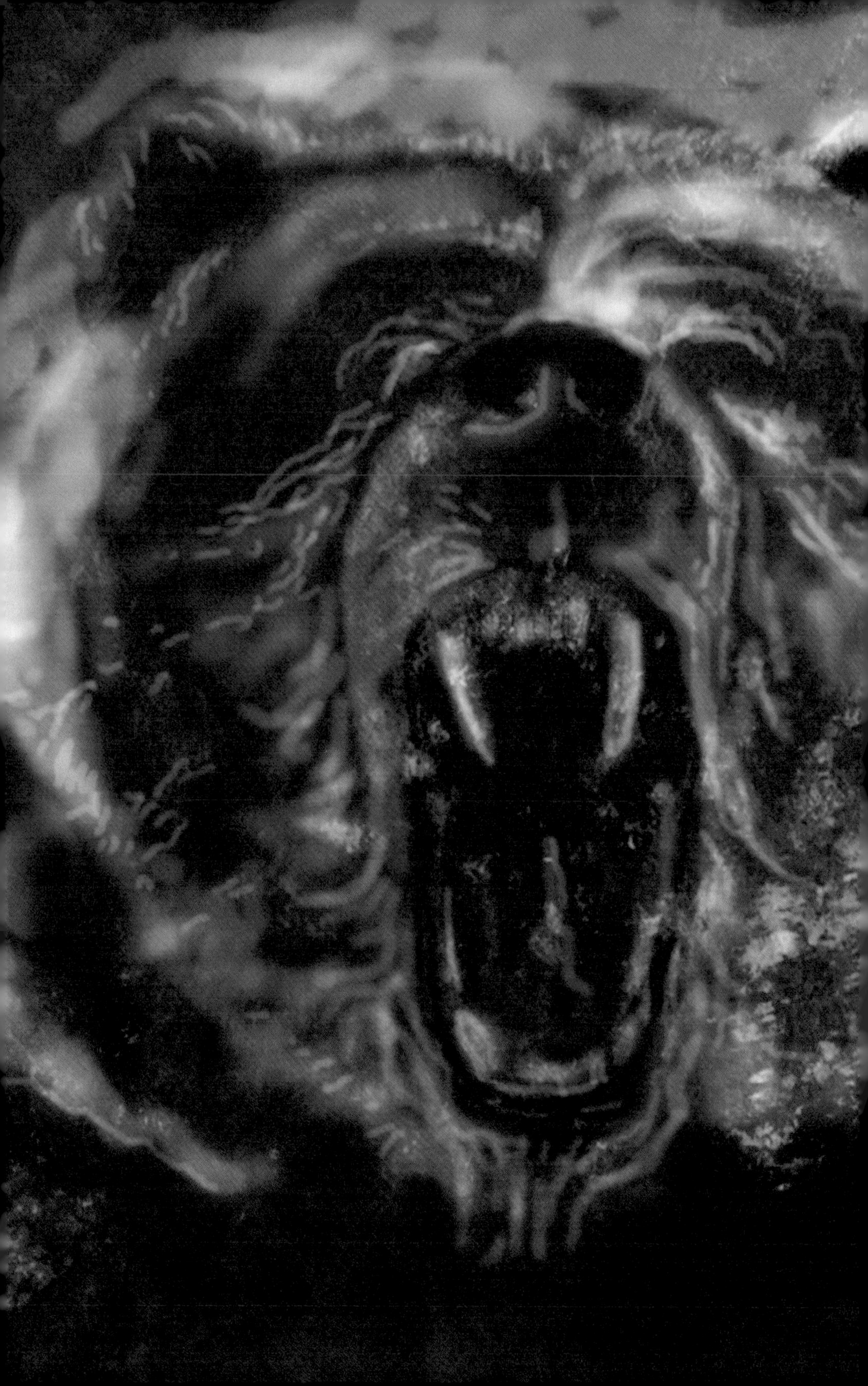

(Beneath The Earth)

It was gloomy inside. He stood, struggling to shut out the sense of panic and recompose himself. A smell of musty, damp soil filled his nostrils, pungent, but not repulsive; it lent the air a certain wholesomeness - a scent of raw, untamed nature.

Gradually, his eyes adjusted. He saw now, just in front of him, a deep groove in the ground. Squinting, he realised that it was the edge of a step. He looked beyond it - several more lay there, leading down into the bowels of the earth.

'*Descend.*' The Voice once more.

No choice - there wasn't any way back. Cautiously, he advanced and followed the steps, each of which was a wide slab of dusty rock. It soon became apparent that they were leading him in a spiral, ever downward. He continued for some time like that, until he began to wonder whether there was any end to them, but still the impetus remained ...

... *Descend.*

Finally, he reached the bottom of the stairs and stepped onto flat, unbroken ground. To his left and right, two flickering torches were set into the walls of a large cave. He walked deeper into its confines and then stopped dead. Directly across from him was a darkened area; as he focused on it, a pair of eyes appeared, glowing in the faint light. A growl, low at first, but growing to a threatening, resonant timbre, reverberated in the enclosed space.

He tensed, and glanced around him, searching for a weapon, and noted a clump of sharpened stalagmites several feet from him. But, before he had time to react, the bearer of the eyes was upon him. He swayed right as a giant paw swatted at him, and something scraped down his left cheek. Sharp pain jabbed at his nerves, clouding his vision.

He dropped and rolled, head-over-heels, regaining his feet beside the stalagmites, shutting out the pain, ignoring the trickle of warm liquid running off his jaw. In one swift move, he gripped the nearest of the thin columns of rock in his hand and ripped it free of its mooring, oblivious of the ease with which he had done so, then flicked it deftly in the air and caught it again near its base, so that it was positioned like a spear, ready to be flung at the beast.

It roared and reared up on its hind legs, towering above him – an imposing mass of matted, chestnut hair. He was briefly awestruck, as his mind filled with a stark vision, of an ancient wooden statue: an animal-god, the jagged strands of its fur like conductors of some boundless, ethereal energy.

Bear.

They squared up, eyes locked, each unflinching, determined and proud. And he found himself speaking again, in the same language he had used with the bird. He realised now that it wasn't his own voice but another; something ancient, pure and whole; a language beyond words, of melody, truth and power. The sound channelled through him, carrying from his mouth direct to the bear, connecting them in a symbiotic exchange that transcended barriers of animal and man. In that moment they were constellations, etched in time and space …

… paintings on a cave wall …

… forgotten but never gone. He was certain that the bear understood – in this instance they were unified, in synch. He dropped the weapon and the bear fell back onto its haunches. And they were separate once more. A burst of sorrow swarmed over him at the passing of that moment.

Everything passes.

They stood, weighing each other up for a second, then the bear turned and padded away from him. The torches flickered and grew brighter.

When it reached the far wall, it rose up on its hind legs and set its front paws against the rocky surface. Two indents formed around them, as if the wall was somehow pliable. A split appeared, running up the length of the rock, from a point between the bear's legs to just above its head. A series of runes littered the surface to either side of the split, illuminated by a faint topaz light emanating from within each of the symbols.

The central fissure grew wider as the rock wall, now two sliding doors, rumbled open. The bear fell down on all fours. Sunlight streamed into the cave. Outside lay a sliver of water trickling off into the distance.

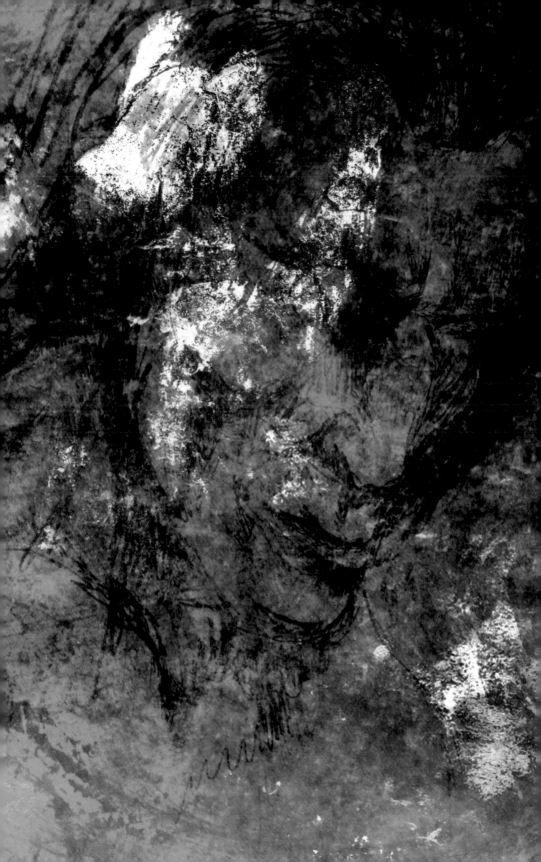

(Streams)

The bear glanced back at him, then faced forward again, and paddled into the water, which appeared to be quite shallow.

'*Follow!*'

He went after the animal. The water in the stream only reached the middle of his calves, allowing him to wade through it easily. Rows of pine trees flanked him on either side, just beyond the banks of the waterway.

Behind him, a low rumbling filled the air. He turned and saw the rocky gateway closing, leaving only an unblemished mountain face staring back at him.

A short distance away, the bear waited patiently for him. They set off again, it leading, and him following a little way back. Dusk was settling on the world, painting fiery hues across the sky. The rows of trees stretched off, forming an open-aired tunnel leading to ... where?

'*It leads to her,*' the Voice whispered.

The bear stopped and motioned with its head to the right. It bellowed out a single, clipped roar, then turned and left, brushing past him as it went. He watched it go, wondering if he would ever see its like again.

His thoughts snapped back to his current surroundings, and he moved over to the shore. The sun had completely disappeared now, ushering in night and its speckled blanket of moon and star.

He waited.

A moment later, a tiny pinprick of light appeared a couple of arms-lengths in front of him. An incandescent blue orb enveloped it, until it was a pulsing ball, growing steadily outwards. A shape appeared within the confines of the orb, faint and indistinguishable at first, but gradually he was able to discern an outline. Before him, ensconced in the pool of light, was a woman.

Oracle.

Her smooth features were placid and unthreatening. She was draped in a silky, maroon garment that swirled about her, giving off the appearance that it was a part of her, rather than a separate piece of clothing.

She floated over to him. 'Be at ease, *Akecheta.*'

"*Akecheta.*" *Yes: a name. Is it mine?*

'Of course, it is your name, as too is it your nature,' she answered enigmatically, catching him by surprise that she had seemingly heard the unspoken question. Her voice had a soothing, almost haunting quality to it – he resisted its allure, his mind returning to the claw marks on his face, a gift from his attacker-guide.

"*As too is it your nature*." What did she mean?

She raised her hand to his cheek. It was like a feather tickling his face. When she retracted her hand, the wound was healed. 'Worry not about these things,' she said. 'You have to be made ready, for the way before you. Because this world is dying, Akecheta, and your time is short.'

What lies ahead?

'You have come this far,' she continued, her voice lulling him, and he found himself drifting off. 'You *know* why you must continue, though you may not remember now. But first, there are things you must be shown. You must look inside, to the heart of all things. I pray that you make it back.'

The ground beneath Akecheta's feet dropped away, down into space. There was no chance to resist.

He fell.

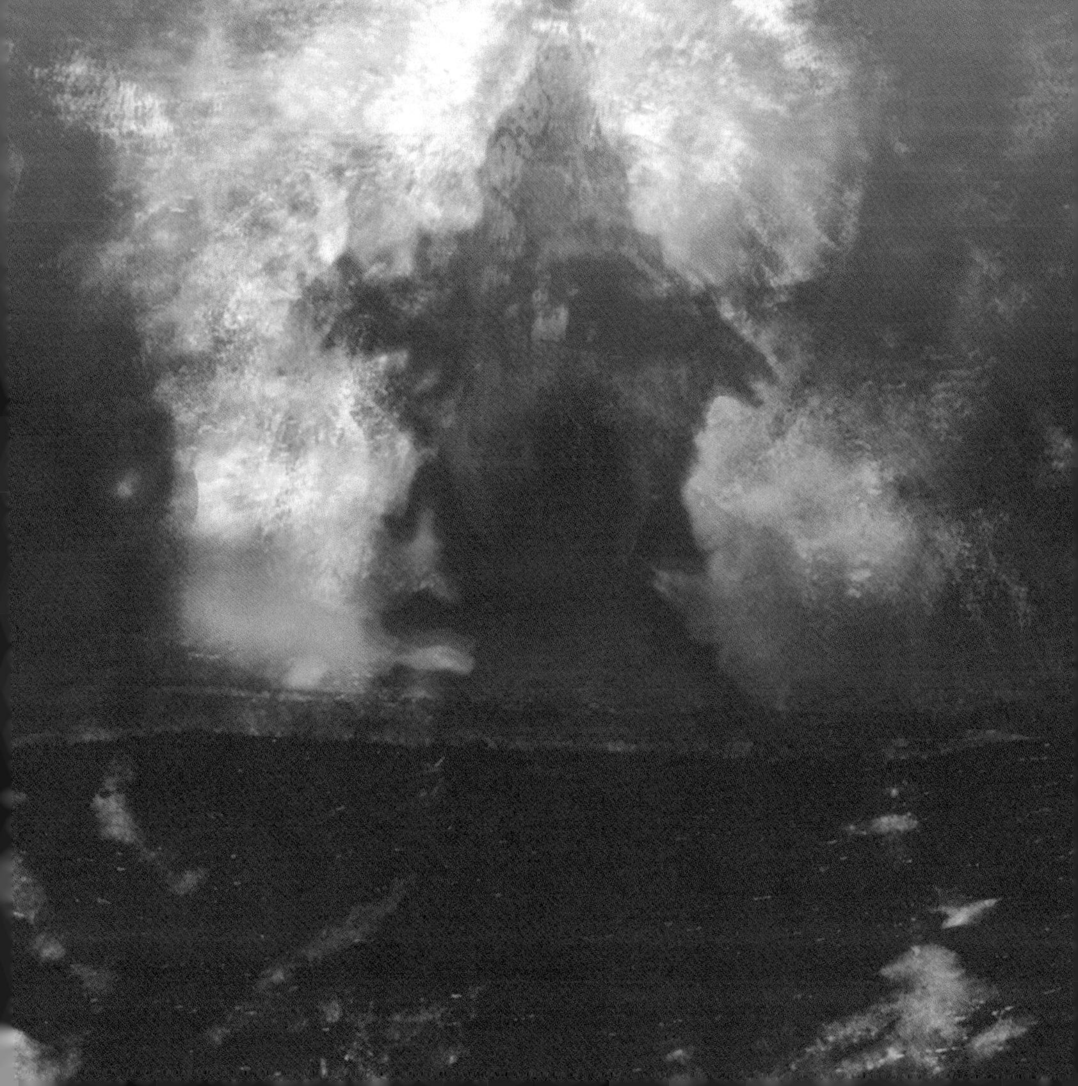

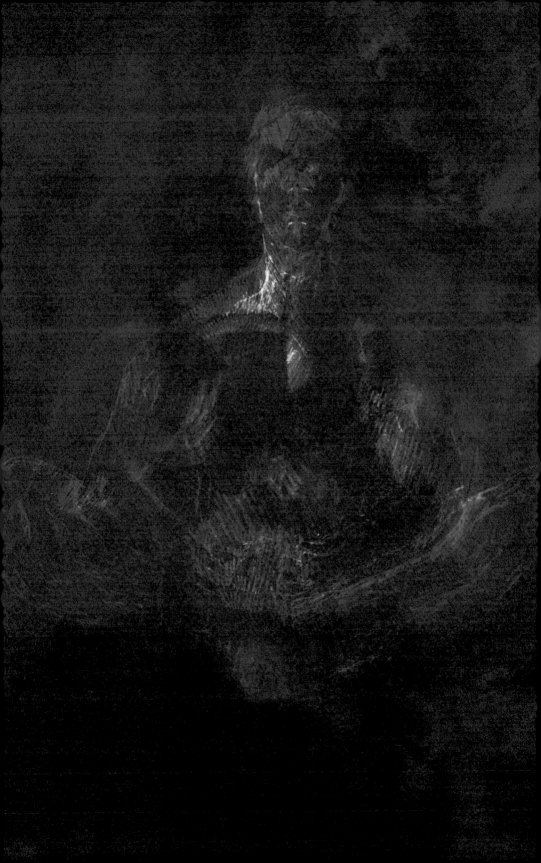

(Into The Abyss)

He drifted for an age. At first it was as if he was in a vacuum that had inexplicably opened onto the world around him; eventually though, all sense of anything was gone.

Akecheta was in darkness once more. He waited for some break in it, some sign of life, but to no avail. Instead there was only emptiness, unending and complete. Despairing, he tried to think of something other than the darkness, and its cold, unquestionable finality. But his mind kept turning to a single inevitable conclusion: despite the innumerable manifestations of light and sound, and of form, ultimately, there was only one truth beyond question; it appeared in his mind.

From darkness we emerge - to darkness we return.

Hope drained from him, and a strange calm replaced it, cradling him in its arms. Like an abandoned infant, he welcomed it, eagerly suckling on it, even though it was bitter and sickly to taste.

Then, finally, Akecheta was at rest. Gradually, he became aware of this; that he had come to a complete stop. What was more, he was no longer alone. He felt it, intuitively.

In the pitch black, an outline appeared, etched into the inky canvas of this void by faintly veiled strands of fire. He could just make out the shape of what appeared to be a man, sitting cross-legged some distance from him. The man had no features at all – the fiery contours only served to accentuate the total absence of any light within their borders. But he knew the outline to be masculine, in a part of his memory that had registered the shape and smell and sound of countless living things, in some other reality; another lifetime that popped unexpectedly to the forefront of his mind, before slipping away just as abruptly, forgotten once more.

Was this a vessel of judgment? And if it was, then what had he done to merit this fate? If he couldn't even remember who he was, or what he had been before, then how could he be held accountable?

Yet he offered no hint of argument, or pleading. He would meet whatever lay ahead with some measure of dignity; no show of cowardice at this, death's door. For he was sure, this was indeed death, arrived to usher him home: back to the abyss from which he had emerged.

Suddenly the dark figure was upon him; its hollow right arm shot out and its ebony hand sunk into his chest cavity. Fresh, searing pain burst through him, and a tunnel of flashing light surrounded him. It contracted, until it was no longer enveloping him, and had become a single thin lance of golden light boring into his heart, and out through his back. Hot waves of agony battered at him, with an intensity beyond any threshold. He opened his mouth to scream, but no sound escaped. He writhed in silence, the pain buffeting him, rising in a crescendo of pulsing torture until it exploded outwards, like fragments of a dying star.

Then a vision was before him, of a vast, open land, lush and fertile, stretching to the horizon, where a great mountainscape lay with the sun hovering just above it. As he watched, the land became dry and the sky turned grey. This was not the grey of rain clouds but instead like vast plumes of smoke, as if the sun had set fire to the grass at the peak of the mountains. He saw them: women and children, their faces sunken, hands stretched out, begging, pleading, '*Please, help us. Spare us!*'

He knew that they weren't pleading to him. Their eyes were turned instead to the sky, but there was no answer, no relief; only the dark smoke.

The ground trembled and a figure appeared, galloping toward them, astride a magnificent, four-legged animal, its pelt the colour of charcoal. Two luminous red eyes glared out from below the figure's wide-brimmed hat. It's features were that of a man's, or more a mockery of a man's; his face was a skeletal, leering picture of cruelty, the skin on it sallow and stretched. He wore a cobalt blue jacket that was tattered and frayed at the collar.

The red-eyed demon at the centre of the world.

The skeleton-man held open his hand - it crackled with an inhuman energy, as if he had harnessed lightning - and jerked it at the women and children. The ground crumbled beneath them. They screamed and fell into a great pit.

Falling - we are fallen.

The earth dissolved and became a river of blood. They were surrounded suddenly by beasts beyond description and scaled, six-headed monsters biting, ripping, tearing at their flesh. A crowd of men and women danced around them chanting, their naked, alabaster bodies turning scarlet as they bathed in the cascading blood.

'*Please, take this from me! I cannot bear it! This is not the way!*' Akecheta tried to cry out, but no words emerged. What small hope he had left in him dissipated like so much ash in the midst of an unending storm. And here, as his mind was assailed by a procession of relentless horror, he longed for death and the solace of nothingness.

At the zenith of his misery he passed out, beyond the grip of terror, and plunged once more into darkness.

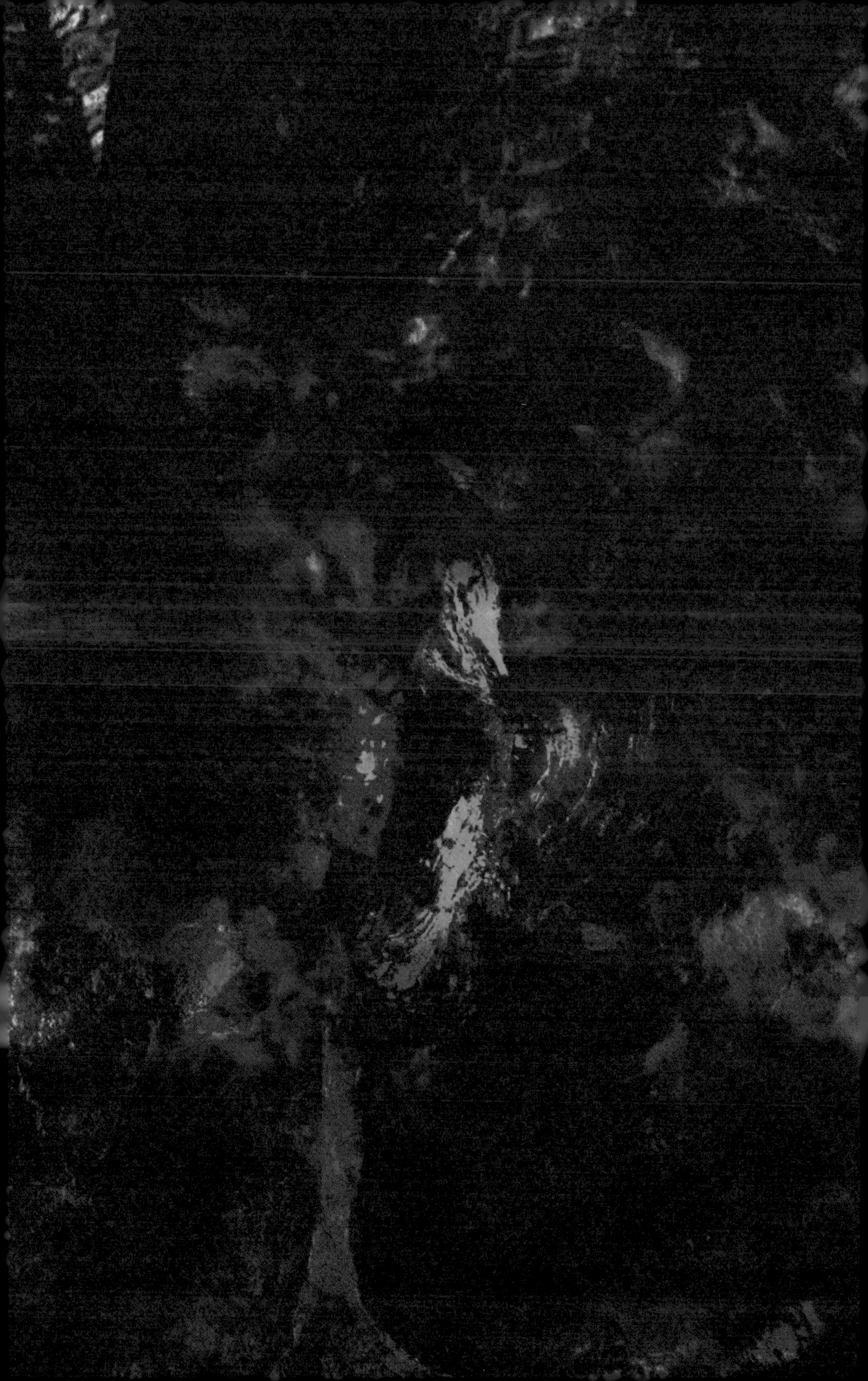

(From The Depths)

Consciousness returned gradually to Akecheta. There was no pain or emptiness. He was no longer drifting. Instead, he felt solid ground beneath him; he was lying, flat on his back on fresh grass. The soft tickle of it against his skin was unmistakable.

He opened his eyes and blinked: it was daylight again. The sound of rushing water carried to him. Sitting up, he glanced around. No sign of the Oracle. He was sitting on the banks of the river. To his left, the formerly becalmed waters had become a torrent, surging off to a point in the distance, where it abruptly dropped away, feeding into a large waterfall, if the roar in his ears was any indicator.

He looked to his right, and spotted a wooden bowl resting in the midst of a clump of grass not far from him; it appeared to contain some sort of clear liquid.

'Drink.'

He was hesitant to obey the Voice's bidding.

'Drink – it will show you the way!'

He inhaled deeply, gathering his thoughts once more, shutting out the nightmarish visions that had been assailing him just a moment ago.

A moment, always lurking, waiting.

Fresh, crisp air filled his lungs, clearing his head. Indeed, it seemed, wherever he was being led, wherever the Voice was guiding him to, it was where he was meant to go.

He climbed to his feet, and walked to where the bowl was resting, leaned over and lifted it in his hands. Drawing it to his mouth, he sniffed it: a hint of pine and tree bark. He drew a small test-sip, and was surprised by how good it was; his throat tingled as it slipped down into his stomach, and he was instantly refreshed. He downed the remaining fluid in several large gulps. Involuntarily, his hands jerked and the bowl fell to the floor, his body spasmed, and he staggered backwards.

He turned and stared along the course of the river, which was now a liquid leviathan crashing forward, tearing at the horizon. Everything had become hyper-enhanced: colours and textures leapt out at him, alive and pulsing, like blood pumping through the veins of a vast organism. He could feel a torrent rising within him, as if he too had a river coursing through him.

Before he could think about what was happening, he was propelled across the ground, his legs operating of their own accord, carrying him closer to where the river ended. Seconds later he was at the summit of the waterfall. There was no hesitation, no stopping – he sprung outwards, his arms spread to either side and, for a moment, everything slowed. He was staring down at a lake, nestled in the midst of an enclosed canyon. The waterfall cascaded into it, forming a rainbow-tinged bed of foam where the two bodies of water collided. The sun reflected off the surface of the lake, mirroring the heavens above, briefly giving him the impression that he was flying up into a rippled sky.

Then the illusion was gone, and everything sped up.

He arrowed into the water. Further and further down he glided; vaguely, he was aware that his hands and feet had transformed, and become webbed, aiding him as he swam.

The liquid he had drunk still surged through him; his heart beat furiously as swathes of water streamed past his face. The light faded, until he was clothed in darkness, as he had been after his encounter with the Oracle. But somehow, this time, it felt right; there was no emptiness or suffocating absence of existence.

The pressure of the water was strong, as he waded ever deeper, yet the weight of it was oddly reassuring, like a pair of protective hands was gripping him, carrying him to his destination.

He saw a dim light before him, and an outline, much like the dark figure from earlier. But he sensed no threat there; no fearful beckoning of oblivion.

'*Emerge!*' The Voice carried to him from beyond where the figure sat waiting. '*Push through. Out …*'

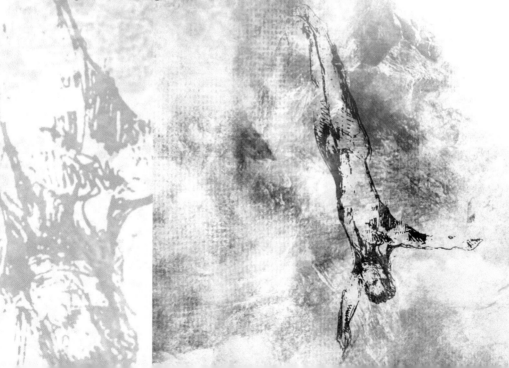

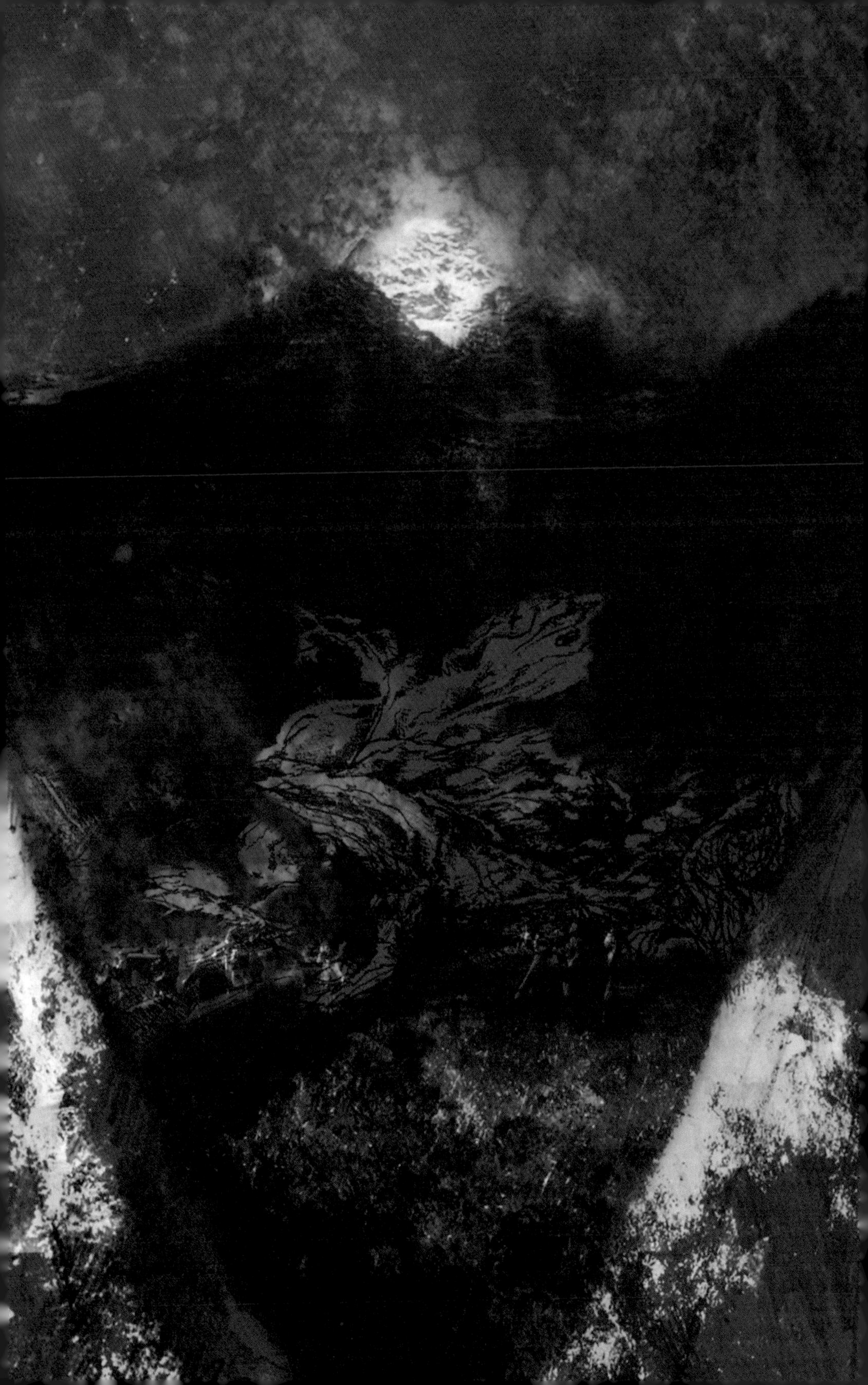

(Toward The Demon)

It was the strangest sensation, as if he had been pulled through a hole in the ground and flipped inside-out. Sickly orange-brown dots filled his vision, before easing away.

It was nighttime once more. A full moon hovered above, casting a magical sheen over the world. He was sitting, cross-legged, surrounded by trees. These were not lush or fertile but gnarled, thirsty wretches, robbed of all vitality, their leaves fluttering to the ground lifelessly.

He stood. Had there been a doorway? He turned and saw only a broad tree stump. A series of concentric rings set into the hewn wood shone faintly with an inner, azure glow, then winked out.

To one side of the stump, the moonlight glinted off a metallic surface, catching his eye. Jutting from the ground, perched at an angle, was an axe with a long, cedar wood handle. Beside it protruded a spear with a smooth, maple shaft.

"*You have to be made ready, for the way before you.*" The Oracle's words echoed forebodingly in his mind.

A shrill scream pierced the night. There was no hesitation, or pause to wonder what could have caused such a cry. That same all-consuming urge that had propelled him over the edge of the waterfall, down into the depths and beyond, sunk its tendrils into him, forcing him to move. He gripped the axe with his left hand, the spear in his right, and sprinted in the direction of the shriek. Wind slashed against his face, carrying with it the sound of more cries.

Help us! Spare us.

Here and there, fallen trees littered the path. He vaulted them effortlessly. Up ahead, the ground fell away, and he skidded to a halt at the edge of a precipice.

Several stone's throws from where he stood was the nearest edge of a village. Pyramidal tents were positioned around the outskirts in a rough circle surrounding a large open area.

In the opening was a vast creature, held aloft by four powerful legs. At the end of each leg was a giant paw. It was ink-black, and had a series of fin-like, vertical scales running along the length of its spine down to its rear, where a long tail swished from side to side. The beast's head was sleek and angular, with two slit-eyes to either side. Three long snouts, like the heads of giant snakes, extended from its face, intermittently rearing up and then plunging into the ground. Each time the muzzles disappeared from view, the earth cracked. Clumps of villagers were gathered around it on their knees, bowing in obeisance.

'*You must defeat it. This is the way.*'

The spear and the axe vibrated in his hands, suddenly alive, as if straining at an invisible leash. He held fast to them and stood staring.

No way back – only forward.

Some greater will than his own spurred him on. He could feel it, above his head, a presence that was him, but not him; a part of him but separate, disparate and calm. He sprang over the edge of the cliff and landed nimbly on the ground far below. Without breaking stride, he headed for the village. The beast loomed ever larger, its massive body blocking out the light of the stars. As he drew near, the villagers whirled to face him, as if startled by the onset of an approaching storm. Whatever it was that they saw in him, it was enough to convince them to clear out of his way. They parted and he sped past, noting the shocked expressions on their pallid features.

The creature's head was directly before him now. He leapt into the air, defiant of gravity, axe poised, spear readied. The monster's eyes, which had been almost completely shut, as if in a trance while it sucked dry the marrow of the land, shot open, now fixed on him. Its foremost leg flashed up, dripping wet soil from several sharp, white claws protruding from its paw. It swiped him out of the air, knocking the breath from him. He crashed to the ground and the weapons flew from his hands. His head buzzed; every part of his body screaming at him as he lay there stunned.

'*Get up! You are stronger than this.*'

He forced himself to his feet. The creature was primed, ready to attack. It raised its snouts and let out a guttural roar, revealing a wide chasm of a mouth with razor sharp teeth. It lifted one of its front legs and stamped down at him. He dived away and the space where he'd been standing a second before exploded in a shower of rubble. As he hit the ground and rolled, out of the corner of his eye he saw one of the creature's trunks hurtling toward him. He leapt backward, narrowly dodging it.

'*Do you remember the hunt?*' the Voice carried to him from afar.

Akecheta looked up at the beast, just as a bird dipped into view between its eyes and sailed off into the distance.

'*I do, brother; I remember the hunt!*' He turned to his right and threw his arms outward, hands open: the axe and spear flew into them. There was no fear in him. He was locked into the present, consumed by the call of the battle. Unbidden, he began to beat the blunt end of the spear against the ground in a steady rhythm, until it became a mighty drumbeat that reverberated and shook the earth around him.

'I am wind and earth and water!' he chanted. 'I am fire! I am the circle! I am complete!' A faint tunnel of light opened before him and he rushed along it. It was clear now, the way. 'You are below! You will fall!' he hollered, lifting the spear in challenge as he ran.

The beast snarled and thrust its middle snout at him. He scrambled and dodged it, channeling some deep, innate animal nature, and leapt at it; the axe arced in his left hand and sunk into its pelt. He used the momentum to swing himself up and scampered along the trunk, toward the creature's brow. It swayed its head and slapped him away with its right snout. He rode the hit, sensing that the left snout was coming up to strike him from the other side; he relaxed his muscles and bounced as it knocked him from behind. The creature was swinging its right paw up to meet him, claws extended. He ignored it. It was as if he was suspended in midair, surveying a great panorama. All the details at the edges were unimportant – all that mattered was his target: the creature's forehead.

The weapon in his right hand felt heavy now, loaded with pulsing energy. He cocked his arm and slung the spear – it hurtled into the beast's skull and disappeared from view. There was a deafening, inhuman squeal and its pupils rolled back.

Akecheta plummeted to the ground. It shook from the impact as he landed. He looked up, just as the demon tottered and then crumpled in a heap before him, sending up a billowing plume of dust. He was engulfed by the cloud.

Gradually, it dissipated and the air around him cleared once more. There was no sight of the demon-creature's body. It was as if it had simply collapsed in on itself and blinked out of existence; a shadow with no permanent shape or form.

Akecheta fell to his knees and screamed a long, fierce cry. Blood hammered through his veins, every part of him buzzing from the thrill of the victory. He placed the axe on the ground in front of him, spread his arms and lifted his head in thanks to the sky, to the full, bright moon.

Sister Moon, bringer of dreams.

He let his gaze slip down again and his blood turned cold. A short distance away stood the skeletal man from his earlier vision. He held out one open hand to Akecheta; he knew what was coming but was powerless to stop it. A fresh wave of torment pounded at his heart. He clutched his chest and his head sank to the floor.

'Tell your people I am almost upon them, savage! My time is nearly here!' His rasping voice sent a chill down Akecheta's spine. It was like sharp metal scraping against stone. 'I am done with this world.'

This is not the way.

Akecheta forced himself to focus, ignore the pain, and grabbed the axe in one trembling hand. Slowly, defiantly, he raised his head, but the man had disappeared. He blinked, disbelieving. *Did I imagine him?*

Before he had time to wonder further about it, a bolt of lightning crashed down ahead of him. The world exploded in a flash of blue-white light and the ground shook. That was when he saw *her*.

She appeared in the spot where the lightning had struck. Her dress was tasseled and sleeveless, the colour of woodland trees. It clung enticingly to her body - he could not help but notice, despite how exhausted he was. Her face was exquisite: smooth and tanned, with sharp, prominent cheekbones. Her long, brunette hair hung loose, flowing over her shoulders. She walked, as smoothly as if she were gliding on air, to him. 'Please,' she said, 'come with me.'

There was something about her, familiar somehow, from a time...

... *when the world was young*.

He looked around him for the villagers but there were only skeletons, lying disconsolately, face-down, as if they had been trying to crawl to him. The ground began to rumble and large fissures appeared in every direction.

The world was crumbling. Starless night closed in, the only illumination left now emanating from the beautiful woman before him.

'Please, come with me,' she repeated. 'There is no time.'

There was nowhere else to go - the path led here. She held out her hand and he took it. A cocoon of light closed around them and then they were gone.

Into the darkness.

Beyond.

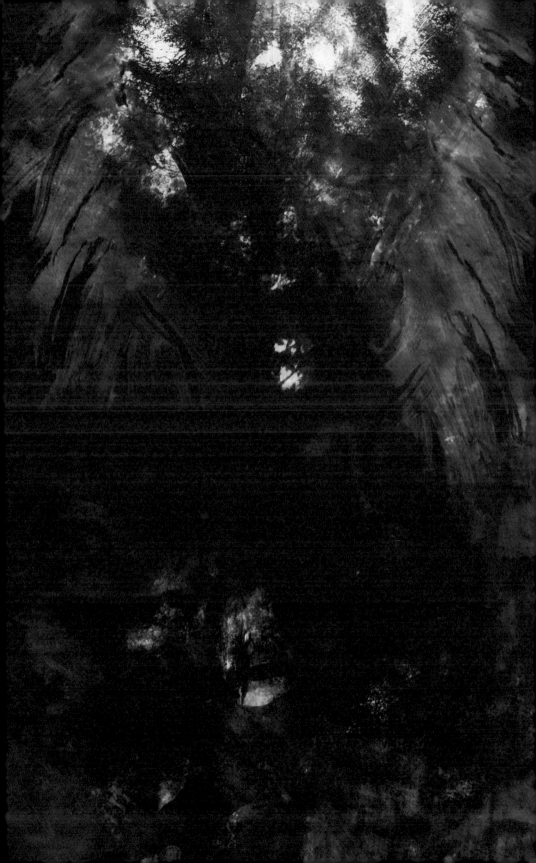

(The Eternal Demon ... Triumphant)

Euphoria.

He revelled in it. They had appeared in a large cave, no sight of the crumbling land. He hadn't seen any hint of an entrance to it. Here, she had laid him down on a fresh, lush patch of grass, where she had cleansed him, using an animal-skin cloth with cool, refreshing water from a large wooden bowl. Then she had sat astride him and taken him inside her. The pleasure had been intense and lingering. Several times though, for some reason, he had glanced around, half-expecting to see the bear appeared again, to guide him to ...

... *her*.

Afterwards, he had slipped off into a deep sleep.

Dreams of open plains, of rich, fertile lands, filled his mind. He dreamt of a river, flowing through a valley between two snow-capped mountains and on to the sea beyond; and upon that sea a luminous, radiant vessel that carried him up into the stars.

Home.

Something was wrong, however. It gnawed at him, though he knew not what it was. He awoke with a start and tried to sit up, but was choked back by a cord that tightened around his neck as soon as he moved. He tried to grab at it with his right hand and found that it too was bound. He strained and moved his eyes first right, then left, and saw that his arms were splayed to either side of him, fastened by vines that seemed to have arisen from beneath the ground. There were further binds around his waist, and both of his ankles.

It was dark within the cave now, and eerily quiet. Forcing away the dread, he focused his mind and concentrated, thinking back to how he had transformed himself before. He pictured his arms becoming two sharp blades, and they began to morph. Yet, even as they did, the vines tightened even more, and burned into his skin.

'Try not to struggle. Please, this is for your own good.' Her voice, so soothing. He couldn't see her but he could tell she was near, hidden somewhere in the shadows.

Then she was on him, her thighs locked against either side of his hips. She sat astride him, naked and magnificent. It was a shock to him that, in this moment of peril, he found himself completely entranced by her.

'The way you fought ... none in this place could have destroyed such a demon. It has been so long since I have seen your kind here. I did not know you possessed such power.'

'Who are you?' That was all he could muster.

'I am that which is most beautiful ... and most cruel. And you, why are you here? Let me see.' She placed her hands on either side of his forehead and brought her face down to just above his. Her eyes bored into his; he could feel her stare penetrating his mind, burrowing into his head ...

Thirsty, pallid children, their cracked lips pleading silently.

The image burst suddenly and clearly to the forefront of his thoughts once more. Her eyes grew wide. 'It makes sense now. I see. So brave, and so strong. And yet, now you have seen *him*.'

Him? Who was she .... Even as the question arose, he knew the answer. *Luminous red eyes, burning like fire.*

'He is the dark path before us.' She lifted her eyes from his and stared off into space.

'Free me,' he said, trying not to sound desperate. 'Free me and I will help stop him. I destroyed that demon - I can defeat him.'

She looked down at Akecheta and laughed humourlessly. 'There is no stopping him. His way is to trample, to crush. Once the path is laid, it cannot be changed. I will free you though, brave warrior. This world is dying and so I must let you go. But first, one more kiss, before we part, that I may remember ... how magnificent you are.' She placed her lips against his - so soft and moist. And he felt something sharp slip into his left side, beneath the ribcage. Searing agony. She stabbed him repeatedly as she whispered over and over in his ear, 'Never forget me.'

The cave trembled and her words echoed in his head. As life drained from him, he prayed for the solace of nothingness.

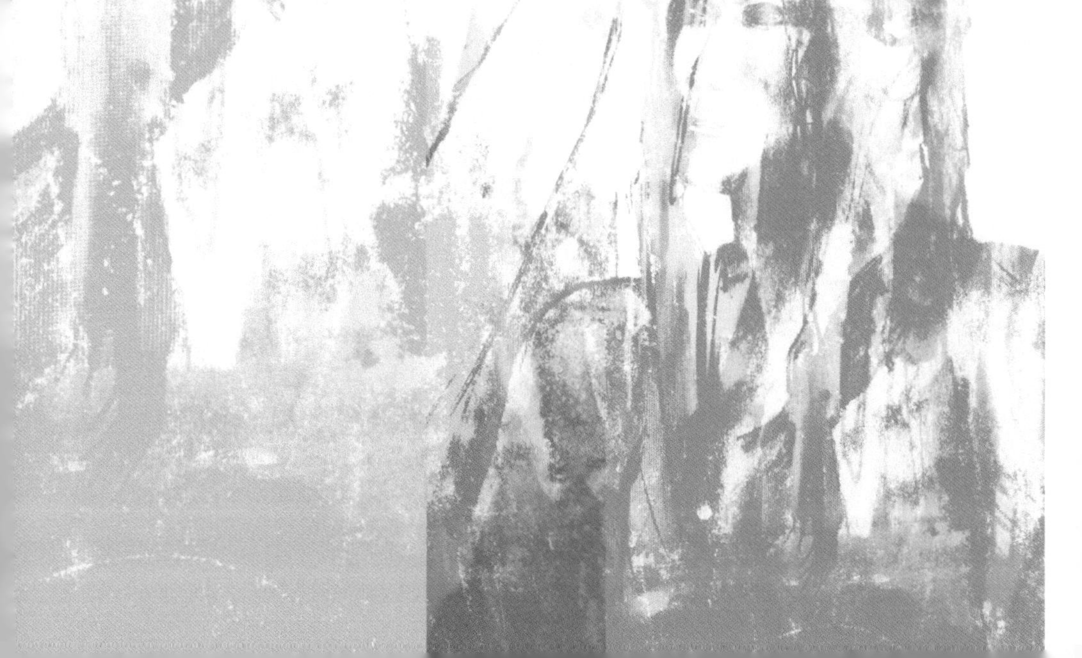

Out

Black, then grey. Mist over water.

Pain had given way to emptiness. Now he was floating, downriver to the sea, and he saw the glowing vessel again. It was like a canoe, but enclosed. He had no other point of reference for it, because it was like nothing he could ever remember seeing. It carried him up into the heavens, to the night sky, and he wondered if he was returning home, to his ...

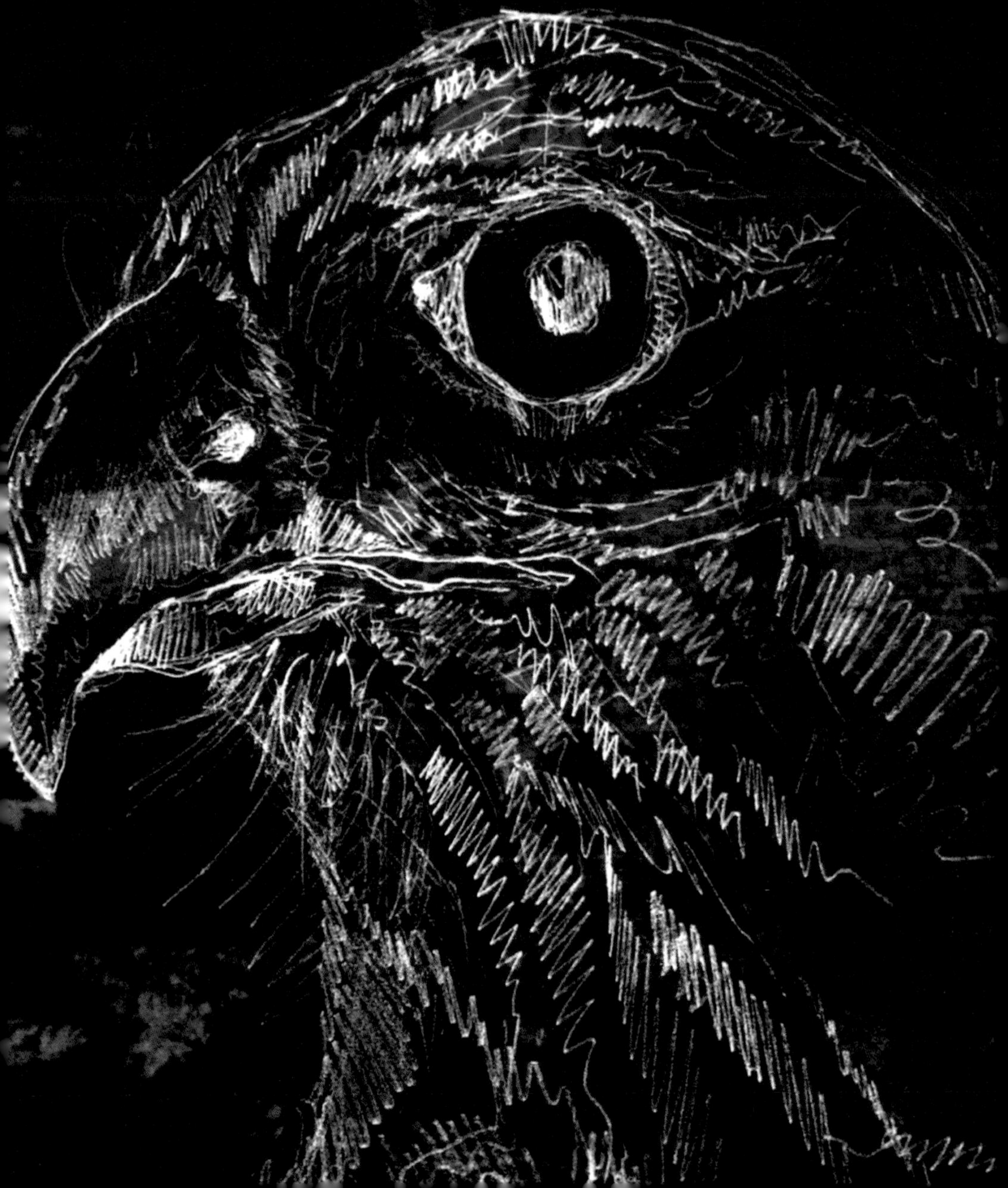

... ancestors.

Yes, home, to his ancestors. Was that too much to wish for? He saw their faces, watching him, carrying him along streams of light, to a star; a star that was ... dying. In whispered voices, they questioned him: 'Did you find it? Did you dream the dream and find the dawn beyond the void? Did you ...'

Sorrow – that was all he felt. It welled up and swallowed his heart. 'I found nothing. Only the dream. I failed. I failed, brothers.'

Their faces faded and he was left staring at the stars.

'*Akecheta, they are calling to you.*' The Voice this time. '*You must return.*' A hawk, its feathers sandstone-brown, appeared before him and spread its wings. '*Return to them, brother.*'

'*I ... can't remember the way.*' His vision blurred. Unconsciousness was sweeping over him.

'Akecheta!' Another voice, barely audible. 'Akecheta!' Louder this time. 'Follow my voice. Return!'

He plummeted down from the sky, into the sea, and the grey mist enveloped him again. He could tell now that it was not mist as he had first thought but, rather, smoke. The smell of sage briefly filled his nostrils before his throat closed.

'Quick, take him outside! Revive him!'

He forced his eyes open; they burned and watered. A thick haze hung over the world. He blinked and just about made out a face; wizened, familiar.

Chatan.

Hands grabbed him beneath his armpits from either side and he was carried, through the smoke, into daylight. He closed his eyes.

'Breathe, my brother.' A different voice, younger, to his right. 'Breathe! You are back.'

You must return.

He forced himself to inhale, and his head swam. It felt as if his stomach was filled with ash and grime. His head drooped and he retched until there was nothing left in him.

Still the hands held him, never wavering, and the same young voice spoke reassuringly to him. 'It's good, brother. Let it out. You are back.'

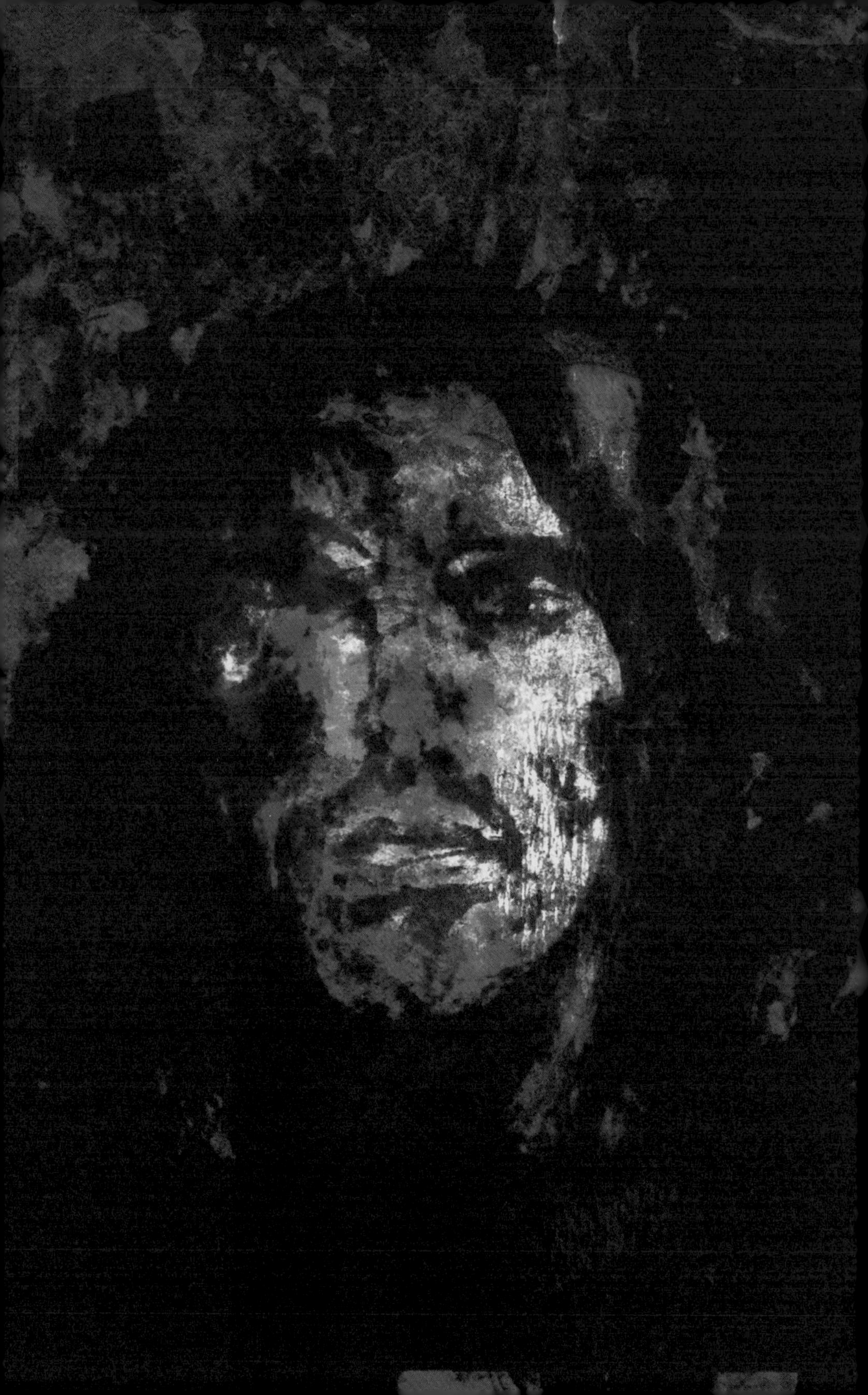

Remembering

He remembered. As he lay slipping in and out of consciousness, he remembered his people: the Sioux. There was no telling how many days passed like that, but he recalled everything. It was like one of the fine tapestries that the women-folk made, its fabric the memory of interwoven days gone past, now unfurled before him.

Chatan, holy man, elder and teacher, who had shown him the ways of the spirit warrior, for gathering power and travelling beyond ...

... *inside* ...

... to the innermost circles of Earth, where the secret guides and spirit totems dwelled.

He remembered the long drought. The buffaloes disappearing. His people moving ever farther afield in search of water, but everywhere being greeted by dried-up rivers and the decomposing bodies of buffaloes, no good to anyone except the vultures.

Chatan himself had embarked on a vision quest, to implore the sky gods to release the rain. Still nothing. The children had suffered most, and the women raised their hands to the heavens, imploring the Great Spirit to have mercy.

The elders had convened. It was then that Chatan had approached Akecheta and said, 'You must journey. Deeper than any of us have ever gone. Find what curses our people. Bring back the rain.'

Akecheta had been on many vision quests over the years since his initiation, but none where so dire was the people's need. The preparation had been like nothing he had ever undertaken before: three days of fasting and an endless succession of smudging ceremonies and cleansing. The warriors of the tribe had taken it in shifts, beating the drums, singing, chanting, dancing. Ceaseless. Eventually all he had been able to hear and feel were the drums. When they helped him into the smoke tent, he had been so disorientated, he had lost all track of time and place.

Chatan had held a small bowl of water to his lips and made him drink. 'Do not lose yourself. Find the way, and return to us. You must return.'

It made it worse, thinking now about how he had failed them, all his struggles for nothing. But, most of all he thought of *her* ...

... *Never forget me* ...

... So beautiful; so cruel. Whenever he did, his side ached. There was no actual physical wound from her stabbings, but still his side throbbed.

Several times, as he lay recovering, he became feverish. Always, someone was on hand to dab his forehead with a damp cloth. They fed him water and, when he could manage it, small amounts of food. Guilt gnawed at him, knowing that it must be some of the last reserves they had left. But still he drank and ate, because refusing would surely mean death.

And still, his thoughts turned to her and her words. He was ashamed to realise though that, above all else, he remembered the suppleness of her body against his, her piercing gaze and soft, intoxicating lips. He could not forget her.

At last, the fever passed and he was able to sit up. He spoke awhile with Angpetu, one of the woman elders, who had been acting as his chief nursemaid. Every time he asked about the state of the people, or how low water stocks were, she changed the subject. He knew this was because she didn't want to concern him while he was recuperating, but the way she avoided the subject made him worry more.

When he was well enough to stand, he wrapped a blanket around himself and walked through the village. The people stared silently at him as he went, making him think of the villagers in his quest ...

... *The lost* ...

... and the bemused, helpless expressions on their faces. He felt like a ghost floating amongst those who hadn't yet realised they were already dead. He returned quickly to his tent.

One morning, as he lay in-between sleep and waking, wondering what hope was left for his tribe, Chatan entered the tent and knelt beside him. Akecheta was glad to see him and sat up. There was a glint in the old man's eye. Outside, Akecheta could hear a hubbub of voices.

'Will you walk with me, my brother? There is something you must see.' Akecheta nodded and, with a supporting hand from Chatan, he stood.

Together they walked out into the cool morning air. The people were gathered about, staring up at the sky. When those at the back of the group noticed Akecheta, they turned to him excitedly and laid their hands on his arms. One or two hugged him. They all thanked him over and over again. He was completely bewildered by it.

'Look! Can you see?' said Chatan, pointing. 'We are saved. You have saved our people.'

In the distance, a bulbous grey cloud hung over the Earth, pregnant with rain. A minute later, the cloud burst and drenched the thirsty land. Akecheta stared in amazement, not knowing what to say or do. He watched as the people danced and chanted as the rain pelted down upon their heads.

The drought was over.

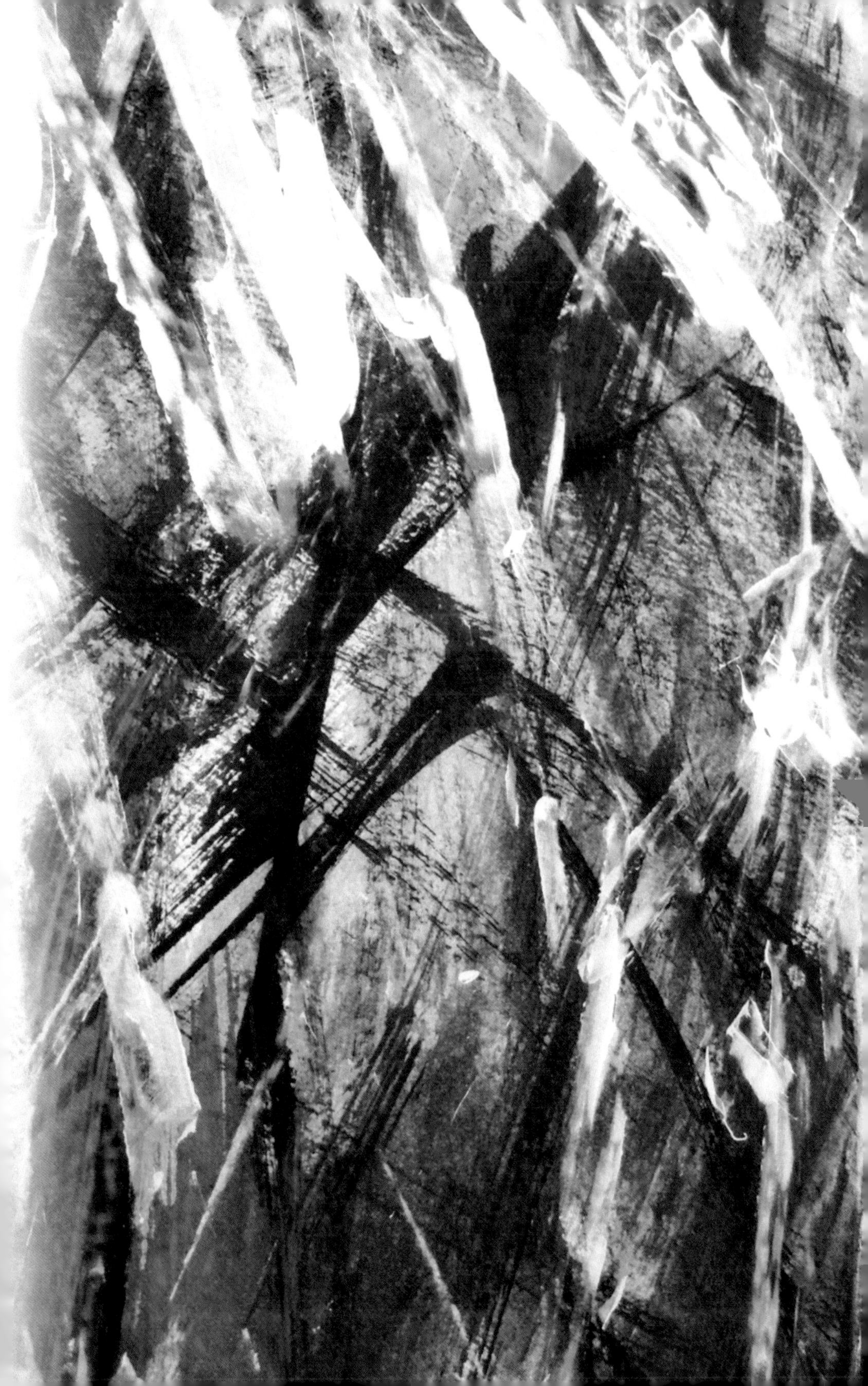

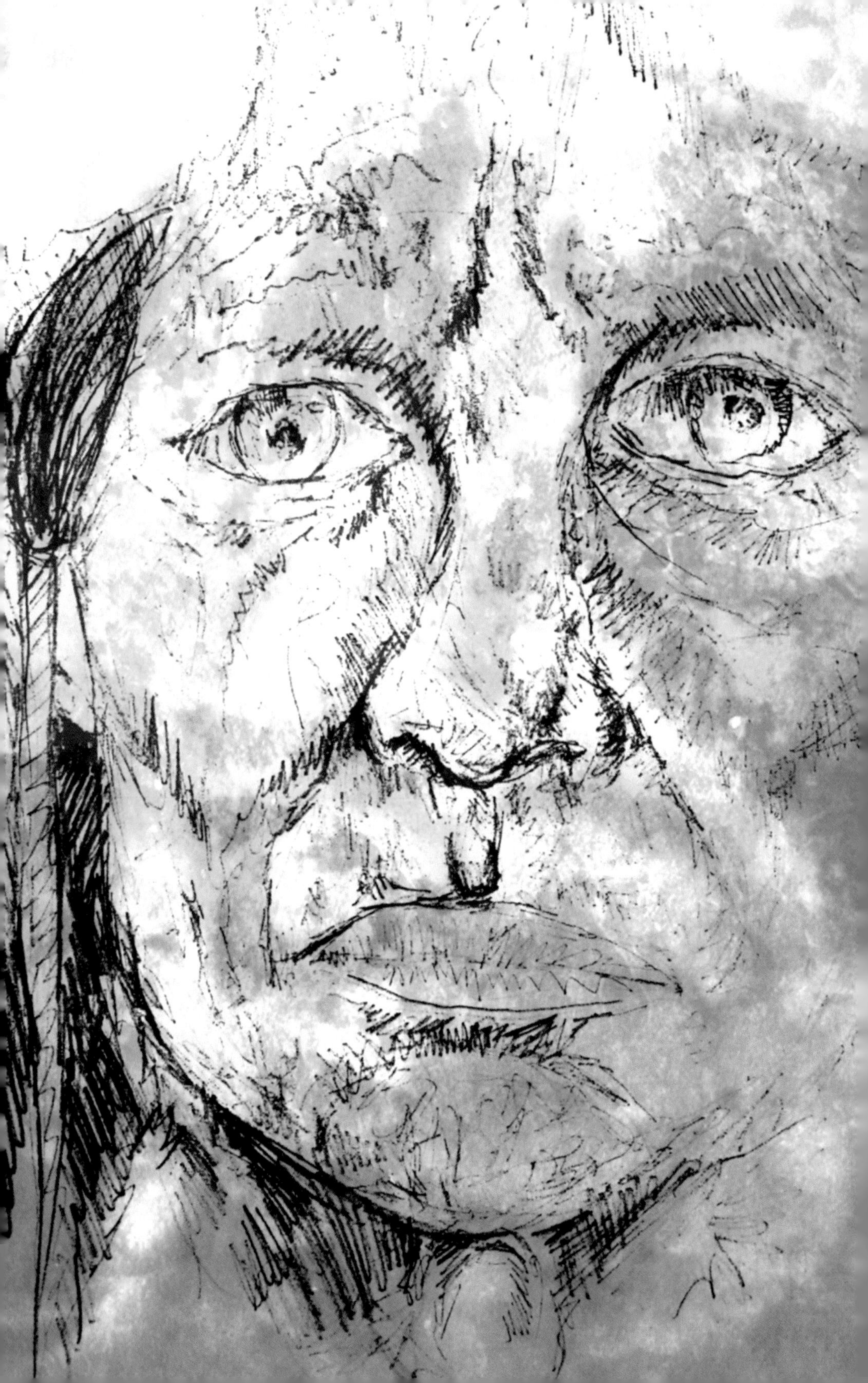

The Passing Of Days

The Sioux flourished after that. Rain was plentiful. The rivers filled to capacity again, and the buffaloes returned. There was food and drink in abundance. For many years, it was a time of great prosperity.

Akecheta was afforded high status within the tribe, and given leave to come and go as he pleased. Often, he would wander out into the plains and meditate, sensing and feeling for any shifts. He was growing increasingly anxious, the memory of the man-demon growing clearer all the time. His nights were often filled with restless, broken sleep, and a deep throbbing in his side.

Then there came a day, when his head felt as if it would burst, that he decided he should consult with Chatan. The elder had asked him several times what had happened on the quest to save his people; others in the village too. But he had always been hesitant to speak of it, and his mood turned dark whenever questioned about it. So they had respected his silence, though he was sure they must have been eager to hear all, still they did not push him on it and questioned him no more.

Yet he knew now, the time was right. It was late in the evening, when most in the village had turned in for the night. As he approached, he saw Chatan sitting outside his tent, stoking a small fire, which crackled welcomingly. It was as if the old man had prepared it just for him, sensing the moment that lay ahead of them.

They greeted each other and Akecheta sat. Chatan lit up a pipe, drew several puffs from it, and passed it over. They stayed like that for some time, passing the pipe back and forth, not speaking. Both men sensed the silence was appropriate, that some greater exchange of understanding was passing between them, devoid of words. Out in the darkness beyond their camp, a coyote barked and then too fell silent. All was quiet now, as if the world had evaporated and left only them there, listening to the secret murmurs of the night as it enfolded them.

It was Akecheta who spoke first, his tale suddenly bursting forth from him in a torrent ...

... *a waterfall*.

Chatan listened and nodded intermittently, the light of the fire casting lines of shadow over the many wrinkles of his craggy features. It seemed an age to tell, and all of it played clearly in Akecheta's mind as he spoke, like he was back there again, repeating it all, wanting to change how it ended but knowing he couldn't. Because that was the path. That was where it led.

When all was told, the old man leaned over, and handed the pipe to Akecheta. 'This, that you have told me, is a quest beyond any I have known. Perhaps it was too great a burden to place on you, even though our need was so great.'

Akecheta stared at him. 'No, it was not! I am a warrior of my people - no burden is too great.'

Chatan nodded approvingly. 'This is good, brother. Always I have known, you are the best of us.'

'And yet ...' Akecheta stopped and looked down. 'The man-demon I saw. He was like nothing I have ever seen. He was ...'

Chatan waited a moment for him to finish. 'He was what, my brother?'

'The end of life! More than that even - something worse.' He looked up at the medicine man.

'Akecheta, you know as I do that there is no end - only a passing between worlds.'

He nodded. '*Wakanda*. You are right. No end and no beginning, great teacher. And yet ...' He cut off and sat suddenly bolt upright. His face went blank and he knew then that he was empty, a vessel channeling some greater insight. But the insight, when it came, was cold, inarguable and brought him no solace. 'From darkness we emerge - to darkness we return.'

Chatan focused on him, regarding each word as they were spoken. Waiting for more. But there was no more. It was all Akecheta had, and it drained from him, leaving him empty, at once too aware of his place in existence.

So small. I am nothing.

'My brother, thank you for sharing this with me.' Chatan placed one hand on his as he said this. It felt so frail. And so welcome. 'I see now that journeying as deep as you have has left you caught between worlds. You must reconcile with this world - let go of the other, or you will never be at peace.'

Akecheta shook his head. 'But what of her and what she told me? Who was she? I do not know how to let go of that.'

'I wish I could tell you, give an answer to all these things, but in truth I do not know. There are many great and terrible spirits in the world below. Their words, often they are nothing. Riddles and stories - they do not speak as we speak. Meaning and no meaning, this is what they give to us. It is their nature.'

'This *had* meaning, brother!' Akecheta insisted.

'Perhaps you are right. But if you cannot find it easily then maybe it is not for you to know.'

'I fear it is some terrible fate for our people.'

'And if it is, what could you do to stop it? We know only what is before us now. This is the way of the Great Mystery: it unfolds as it will.'

Akecheta considered this briefly. 'I know that you are right. Still, I wish that I could return there to find the meaning of this - to fix it.'

'Do you think you could return, then?'

The question hung in the air between them and Akecheta wondered. The answer however, was quickly evident. 'No. That world was disappearing when I ... when *she* forced me out.'

'It seems that this saved you, yes? If you hadn't been forced out, I wonder if you would have found the way back yourself.'

'So you are saying that stabbing me was a good thing?'

Chatan laughed. 'Well, it worked, so I guess it was necessary. Sometimes the extreme way is the only way.'

'So *this* is the wisdom of my revered teacher?'

They looked at each other and both smiled. Then Chatan grew serious again and said, 'Do you know why you were chosen for this task, to save us?'

Akecheta shook his head. 'No. I did only as asked, because it fell to me.'

'Of course. But you should understand. Listen to me a moment. You see, when we were at our most desperate, when all had failed, I communed with the ancestors, and they showed me you, and your true nature.' He paused, drew a deep puff of smoke, and let it stream out from the corner of his mouth. 'When our ancestors travelled long ago to this land, from across the world, they were led by the great dreamers, because they knew not the way. These were the ones who dreamt the unknown, striding forward into the emptiness. They found the way where others could not. In you is the spirit of these great ancestors, the last of this kind among us. Know that only you could have done as you did.'

Akecheta stared at Chatan, trying to digest and comprehend what he had just been told. He must have appeared doubtful because the holy man leaned over and gently squeezed his hand. 'My brother, dwell not on these things that have passed. Make peace with this world and enjoy your remaining time in this life, before your spirit passes back to the ancestors. You have saved us, and this is good.'

Akecheta forced a smile and nodded in appreciation. Silently though, he remained unconvinced, and wondered about what was to come, and the invisible wound in his side.

The wound never healed.

The Endless Night

That night, Akecheta opened his eyes. It was one of the rare occasions when he hadn't been dreaming, so he wasn't sure what had caused him to wake.

'*Follow.*' It was the Voice, his guide, soft and distant, but he was sure of it.

Strange, he thought, that he should hear it now, outside of a dream quest. He had not heard it since his fateful journey.

'*Follow,*' it repeated.

He stood and exited his tent. The moon was full and the sky cloudless. Nothing stirred.

'*They are waiting. Follow.*'

He focused on the moon and now he was sure, he saw a path of light cascading down from it, leading off into the wilderness. He wandered away from the camp, following it. He had done such things before - for the spirit warrior the call of night was powerful. But this felt different - everything was so still, as if all the world were asleep and he was the only one there, wandering in the landscape of their dreams.

The long grass brushed against his thighs as he walked, not knowing where he was going but instinctively following.

He stopped. The wind had picked up, and rustled through the grass, whispering ...

'*Here, Akecheta. They are here.*'

He sat and stared up at the sky. '*Wakan-Tanka. I have dreamed the dream. Show me the way, beyond the void.*'

Before his eyes, the stars shifted and formed into the faces of his ancestors ...

... those he did not recognise and, yet, they were more familiar to him than the faces of any others he had known in his life. He saw tears, streams of golden light, trickling down their faces.

'*Why do you weep? All is well. Our people are saved.*'

'*We weep because we see now, brother.*' Their voices soft, far away, carried on the wind. '*We have seen the dawn. You have shown us the way. We weep because we see.*'

And even as Akecheta stared up at them, he too began to weep.

Because he saw.

Dreaming The Unknown

He dreamt of her.

In the distance, beneath the setting sun, stood a mesa. At its foot, buffaloes grazed while clumps of villagers – his people – danced about them, their feet sending up puffs of dust as they stamped in time to the rhythm of the drummers. The buffaloes had no fear of them; there was no hunting here: all had plenty, and they were content with that.

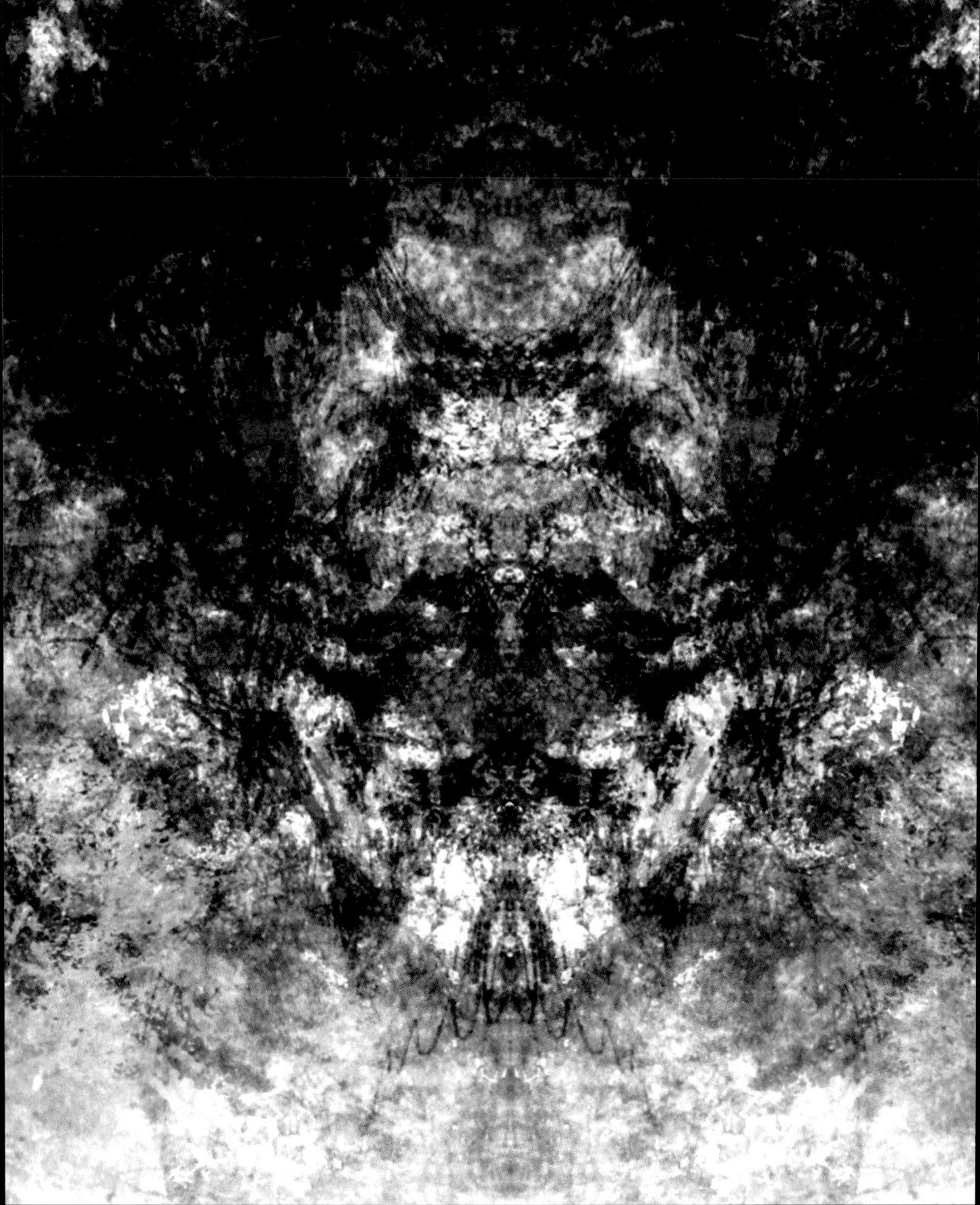

She appeared from nowhere, an apparition, made manifest from the mists of whatever world she called home, and strode to him. He lusted for her, yearned for the feel of her long legs wrapped around him once more.

As she reached him, she planted a moist kiss upon his lips. He leaned in but she yanked away, and he felt a familiar sharp pain in his side, where she had stabbed him before; where she stabbed him again and again. Still, he yearned for her, unable to quell his maddening lust. He fell to his knees, blood seeping from where the blade had pierced.

She stepped away, fixing him with sorrowful eyes. 'I am sorry, brave warrior.'

On the horizon, a storm cloud gathered, blotting out all sun. Lightning jagged into the earth haphazardly, casting away the darkness in nightmarish, sporadic flashes.

Then Akecheta saw him, a terrifying vision of unfettered hatred upon his steed. His eyes were like two embers beneath the brim of his wide hat, long silver hair billowing out to either side of it. In his left hand, he wielded a long chain with shackles that hung loose at his side, clanging and crashing against the ground as he galloped forward. In his right hand was a great, metallic stick.

He drove into the midst of the people. The buffaloes scattered but, as they fled, he shot them down with bursts of lightning from his metal stick: every repetition from it echoed across the valley, more terrifying than the sound of any thunder.

'Bow before me, savages!' he boomed, his voice all malice and sneering cruelty. 'Bow and yield ... or perish!'

Still, even in the face of this terrible foe, the Sioux warriors strode forward proudly, tomahawks in hand. His steed reared up, its forelegs punching at the empty air. From behind him, an army rode forth, each of the soldiers a precise copy of him. The warriors rushed to meet them. They clashed, metal against metal. Some of the warriors managed to wrestle away a few of the thunder sticks, and struck down their assailants. But even as they did, still more of the men-demons joined the battle. His people began to falter in the face of this endless onslaught.

And all the while, as the two forces clashed, the leader of these unholy assailants perched arrogantly atop his mount, grinning and licking his lips. Akecheta forced his eyes away and sought her out. She stood off to the side of the clashes and he saw that she had chains around her neck. 'Never forget me,' she whispered.

The dark cloud above the masa burst,

bringing with it not a torrent of rejuvenating rain,

but a flood of surging, bloody water,

carrying the carcasses of fallen men and animals

There was nothing he could do to hold it back,
that murderless flood.

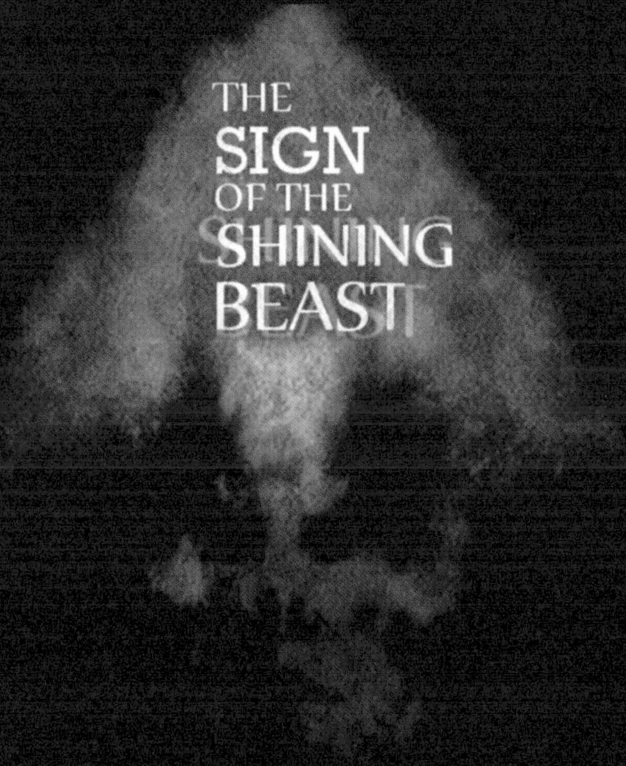
THE SIGN OF THE SHINING BEAST

At
night
I dream
the endless
sleep

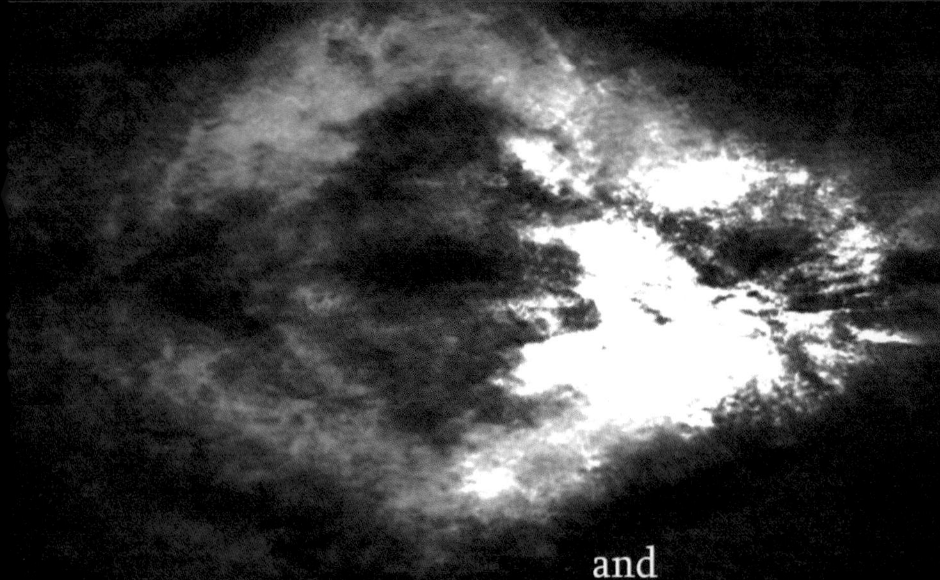

and
it
always
begins ends
as
it
ends begins

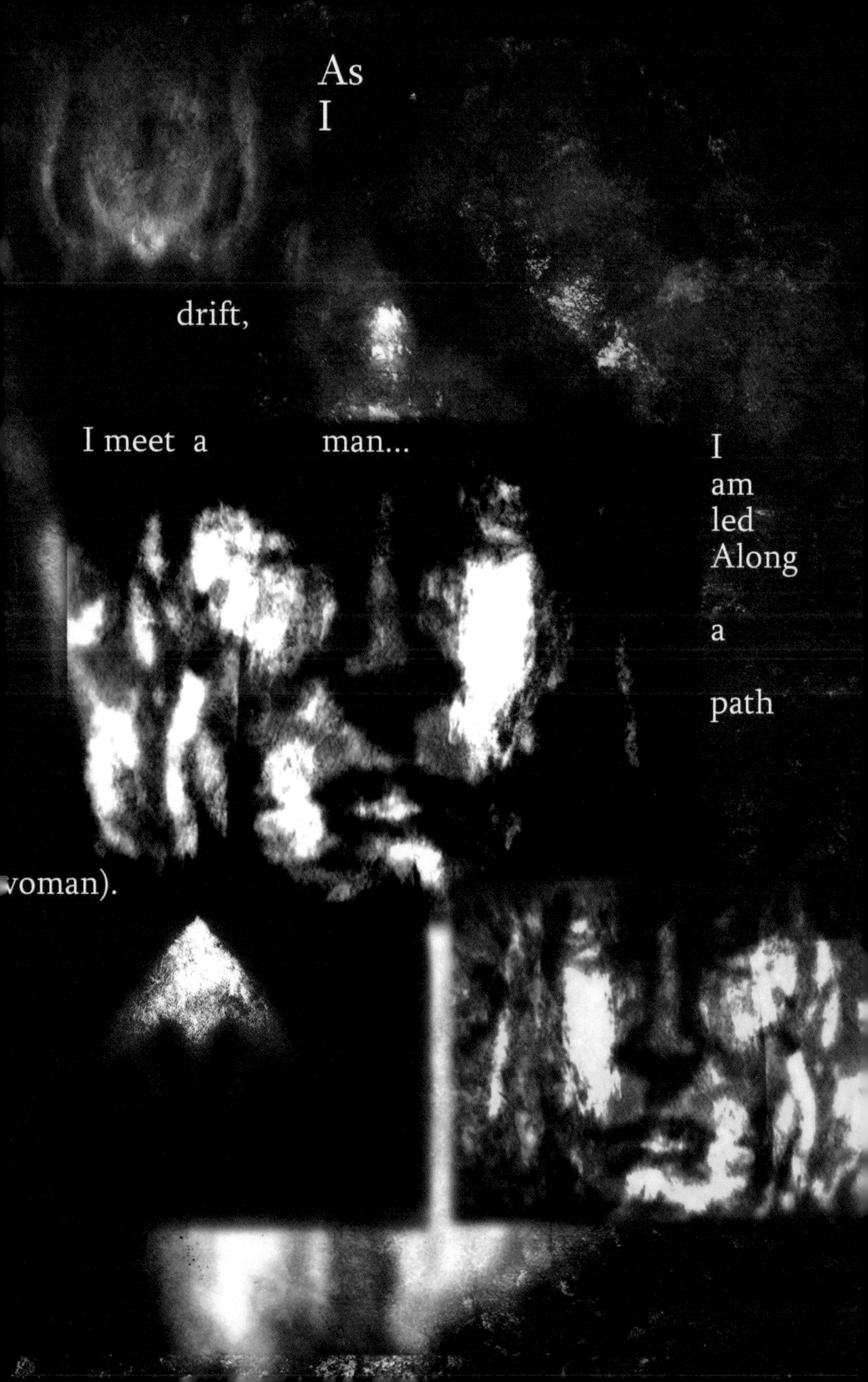

As
I

drift,

I meet a man...

I
am
led
Along
a
path

voman).

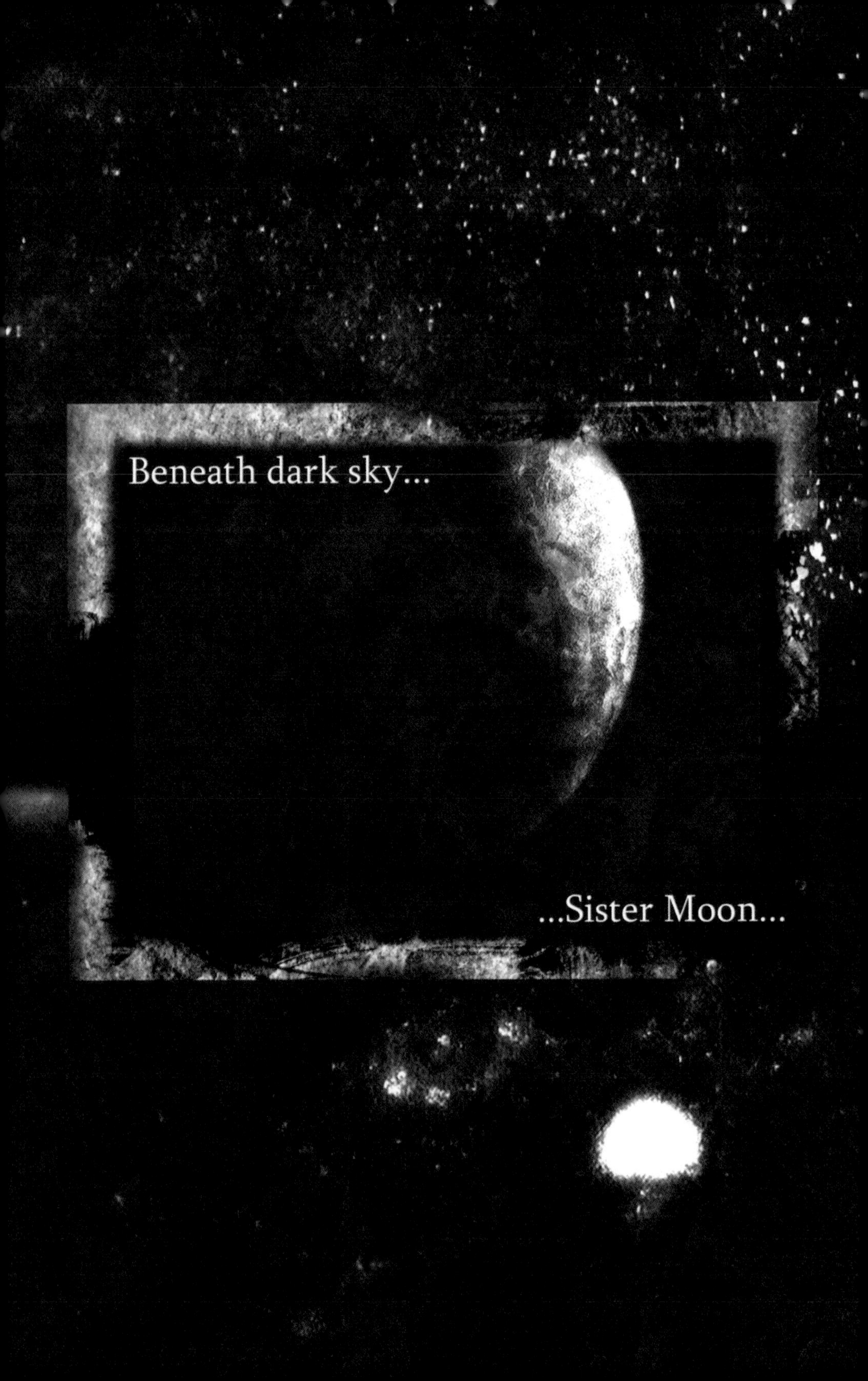
Beneath dark sky...
...Sister Moon...

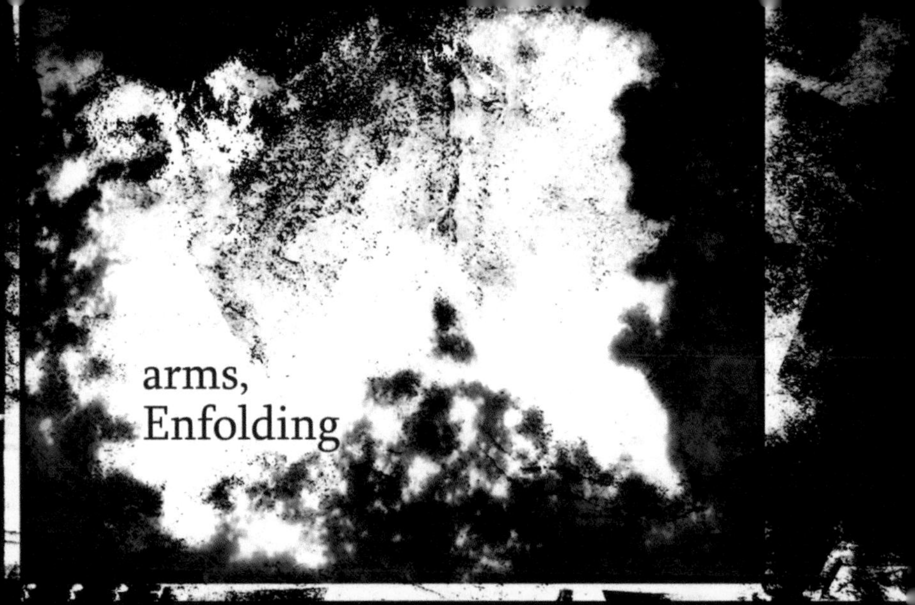

Trees like arms,
Enfolding

A clearing. A moonlit sky.

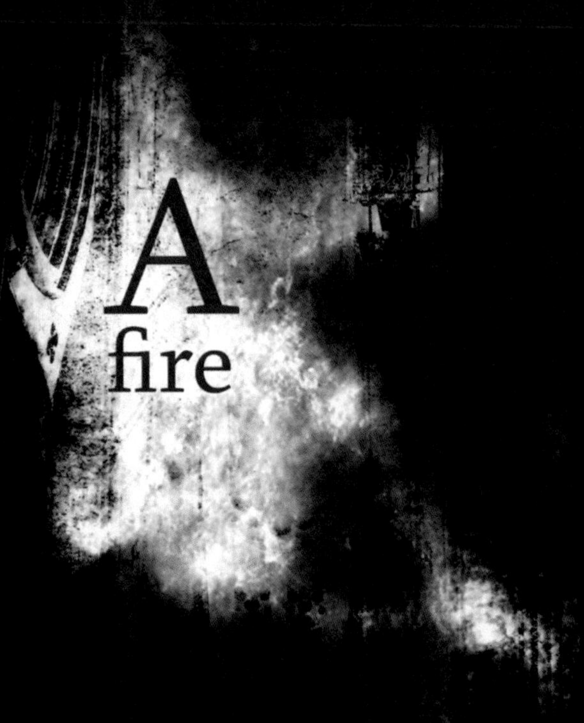

A
fire

in endless night.

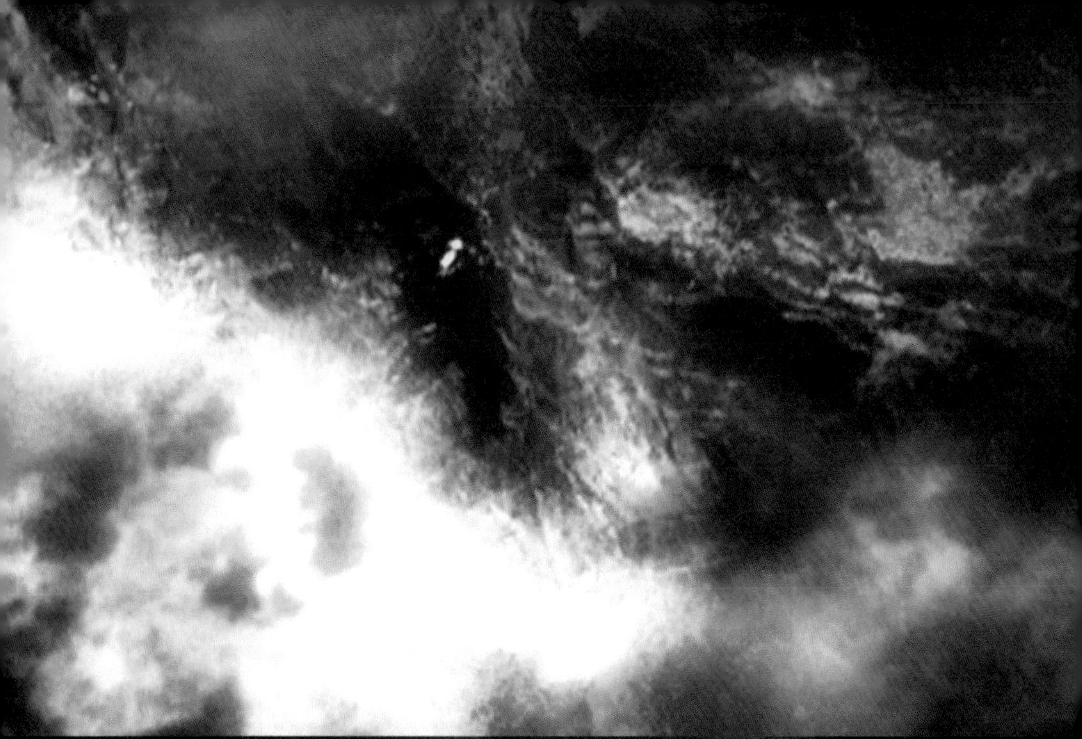

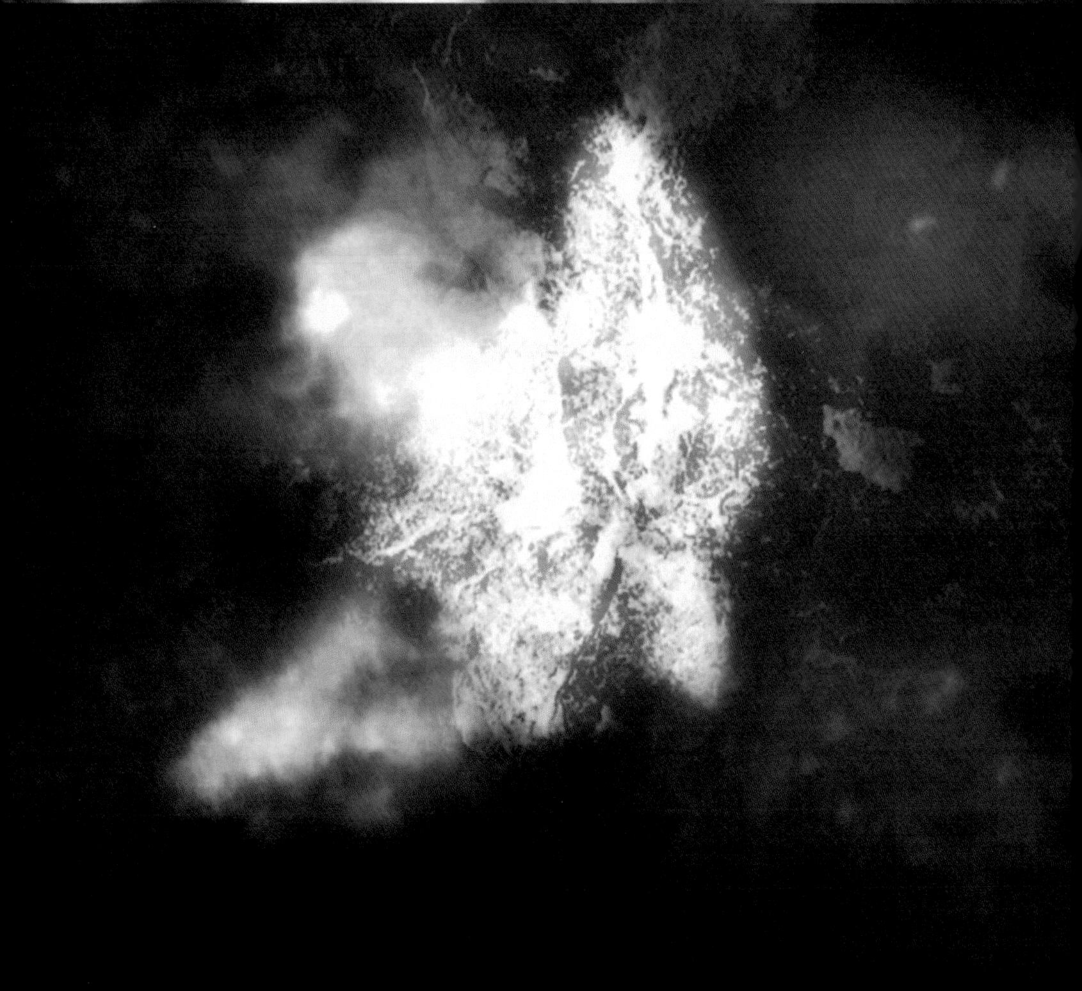

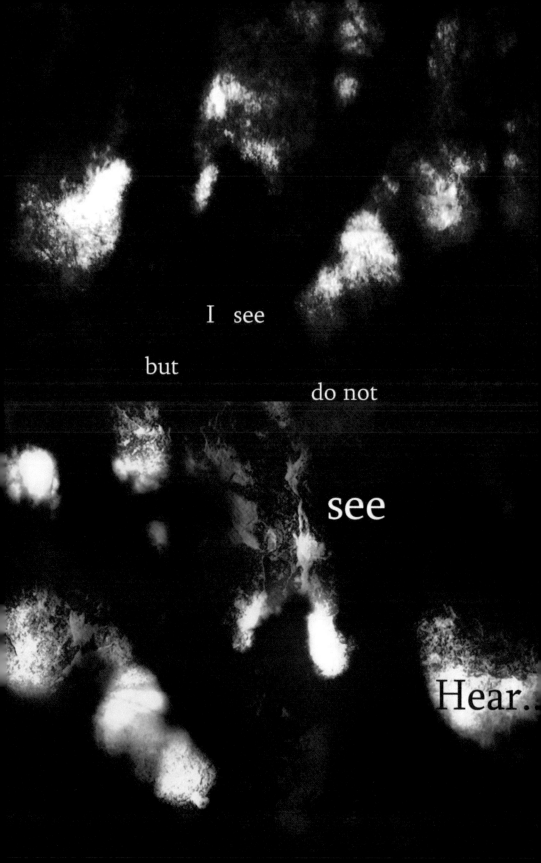

I see

but

do not

see

Hear..

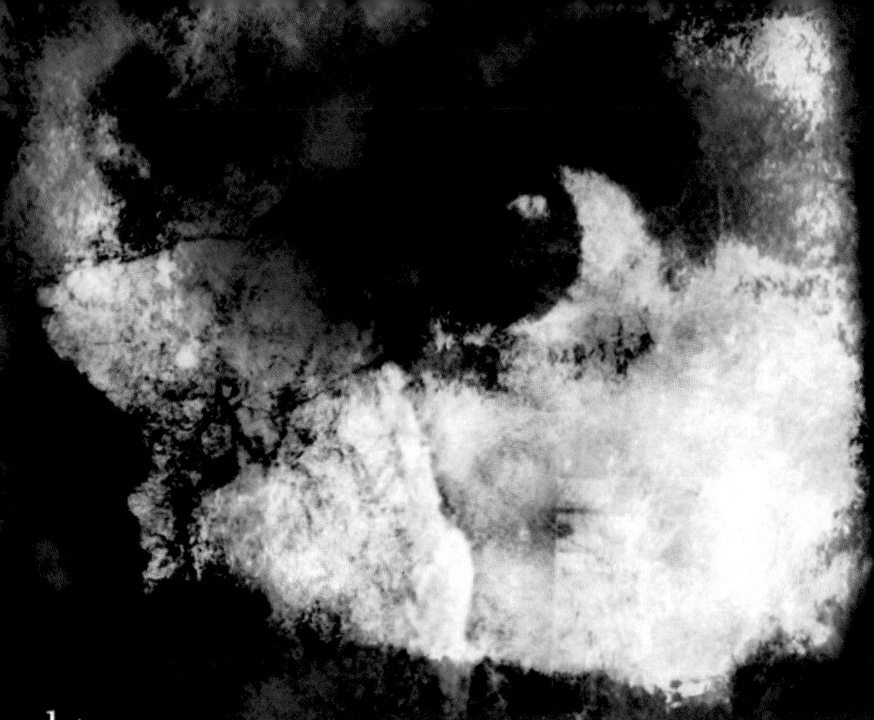

...laughter

Innocent

Forgotten

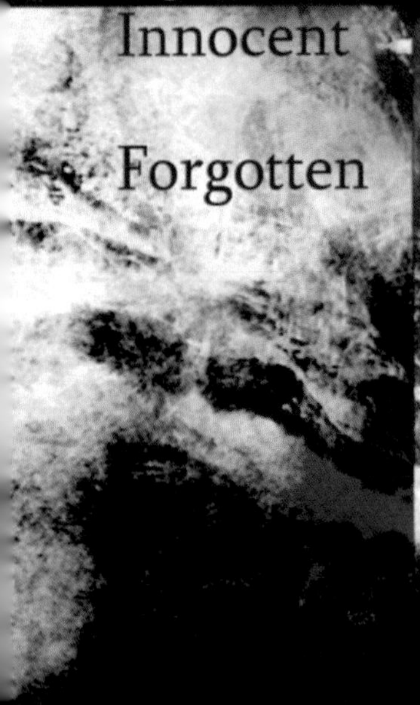

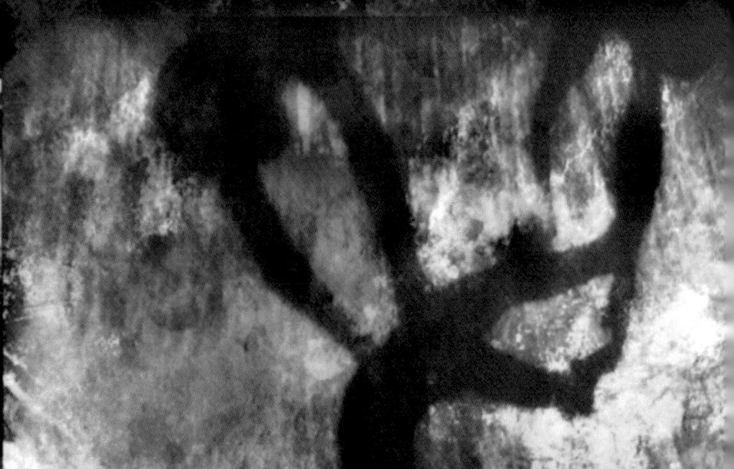

Was there a day?
A
time
for
play?

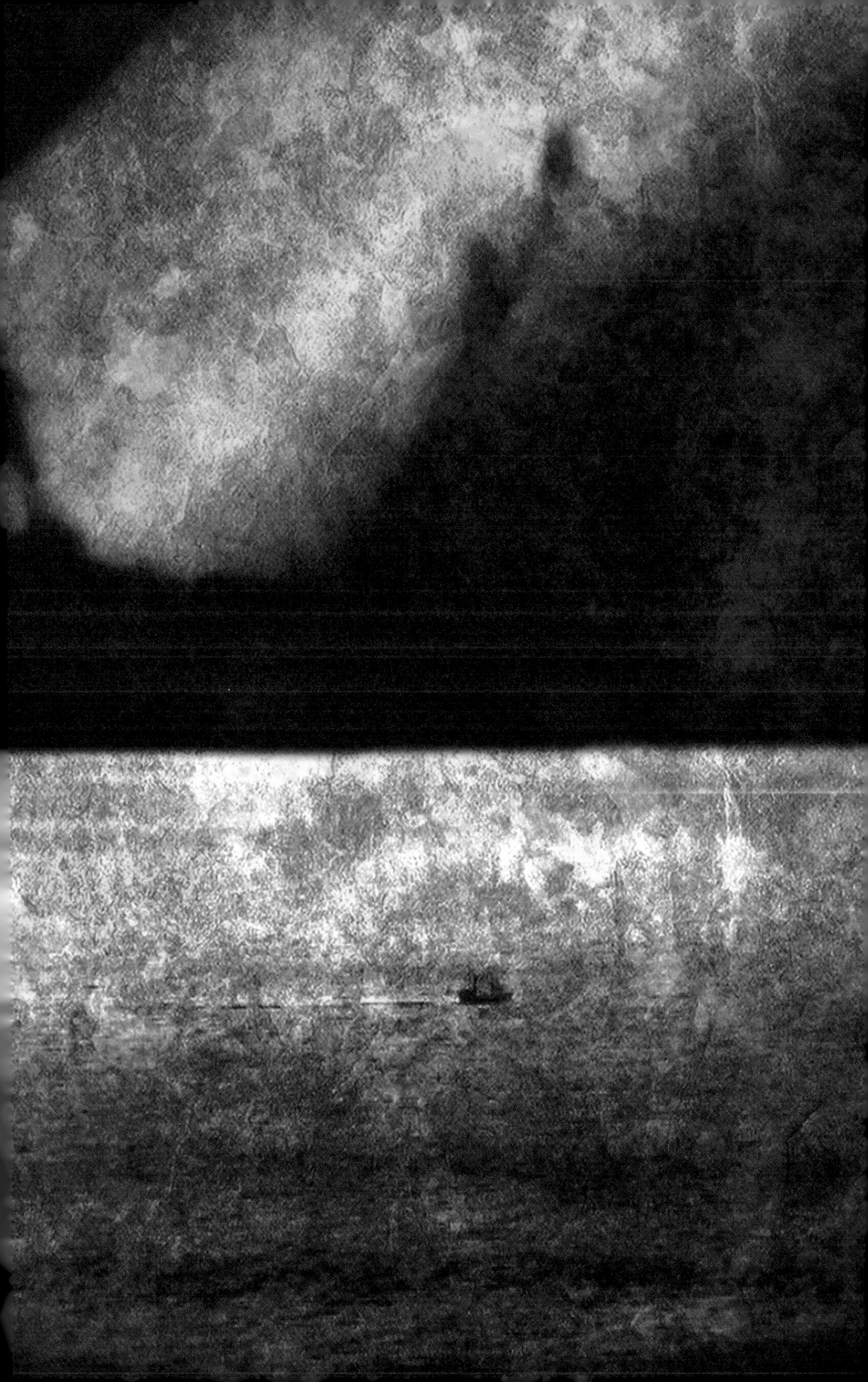

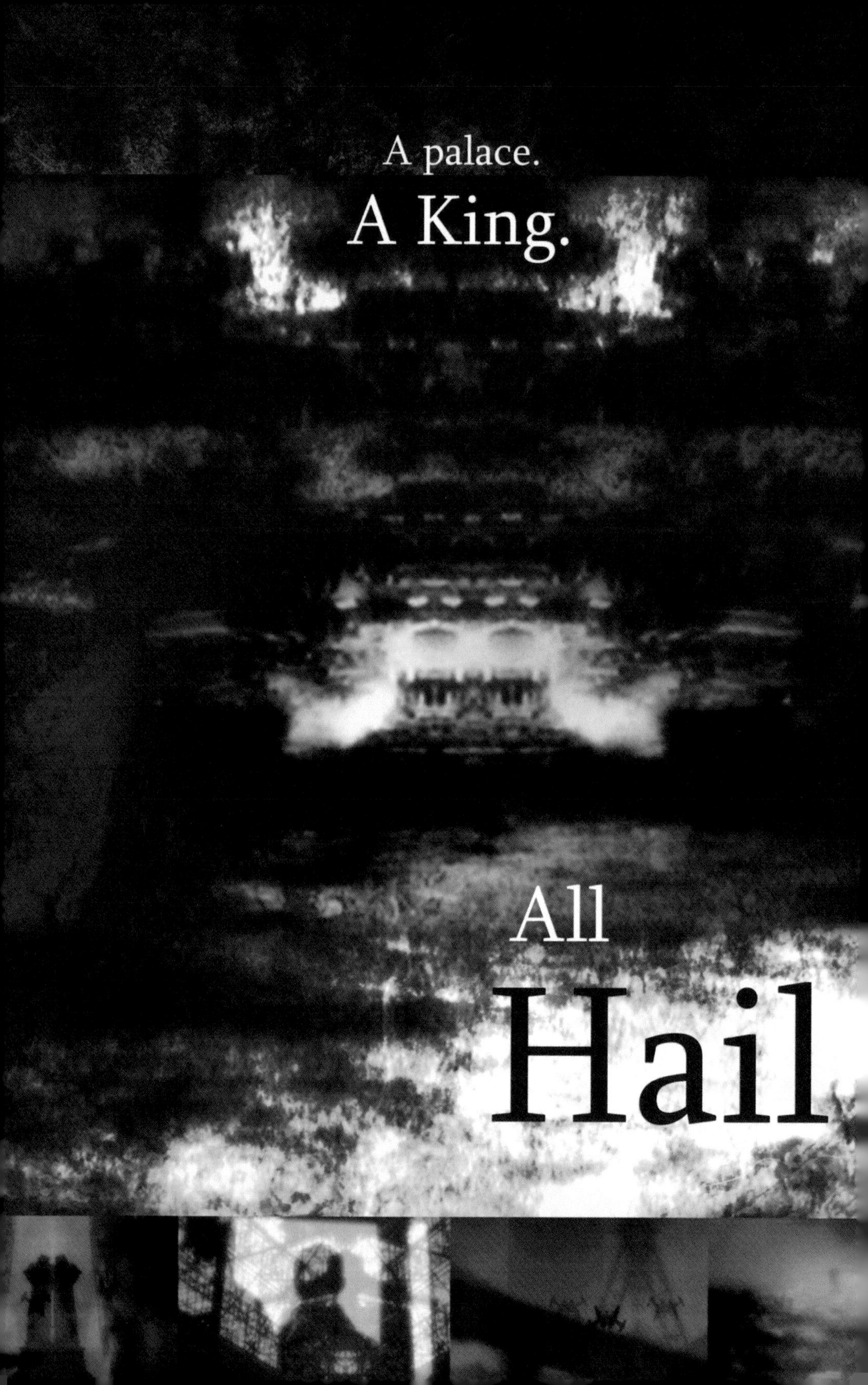
A palace.
A King.
All
Hail

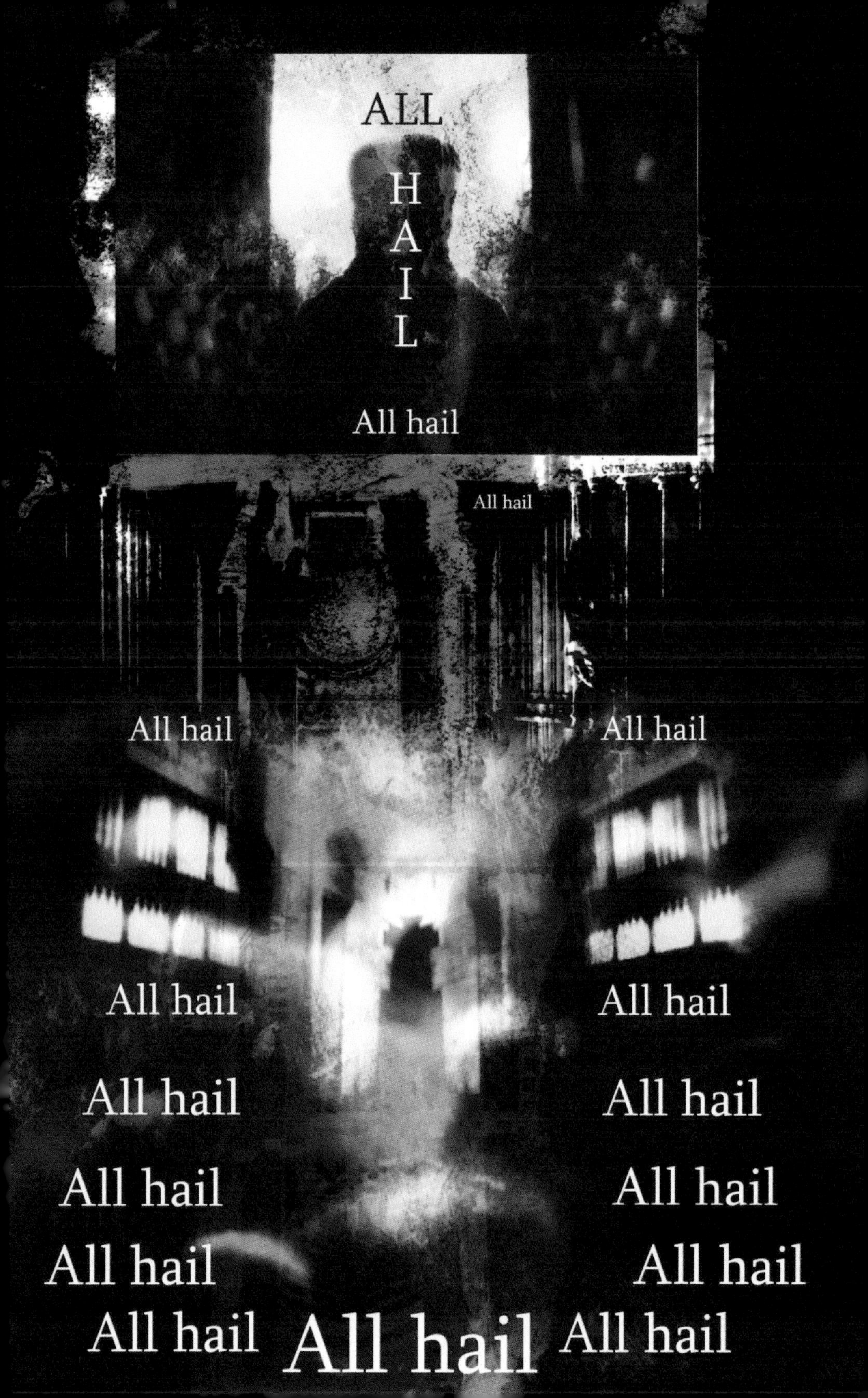
ALL
H
A
I
L
All hail
All hail
All hail
All hail
All hail
All hail
All hail
All hail
All hail
All hail
All hail
All hail
All hail
All hail
All hail

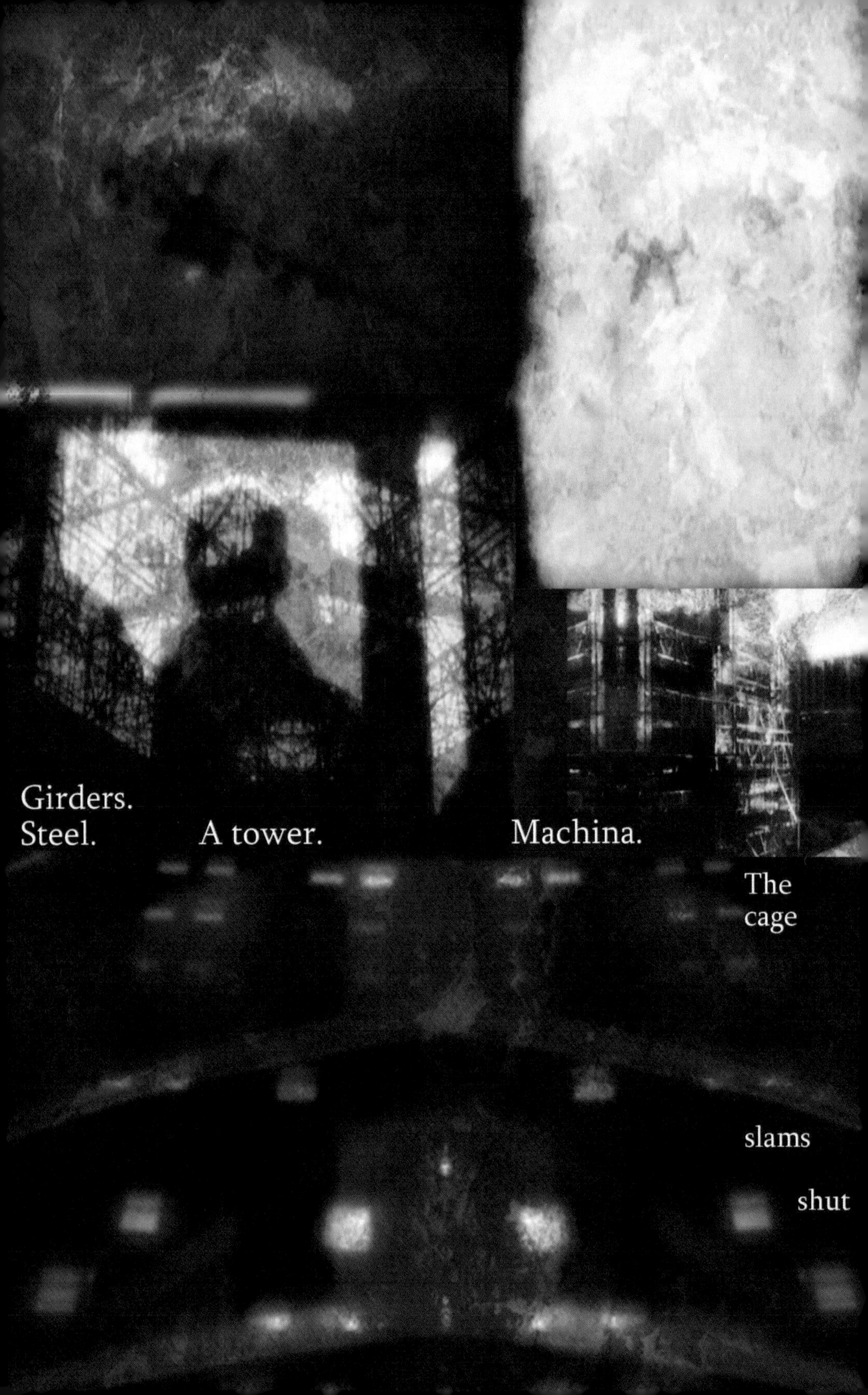
Girders.
Steel.
A tower.
Machina.
The cage
slams
shut

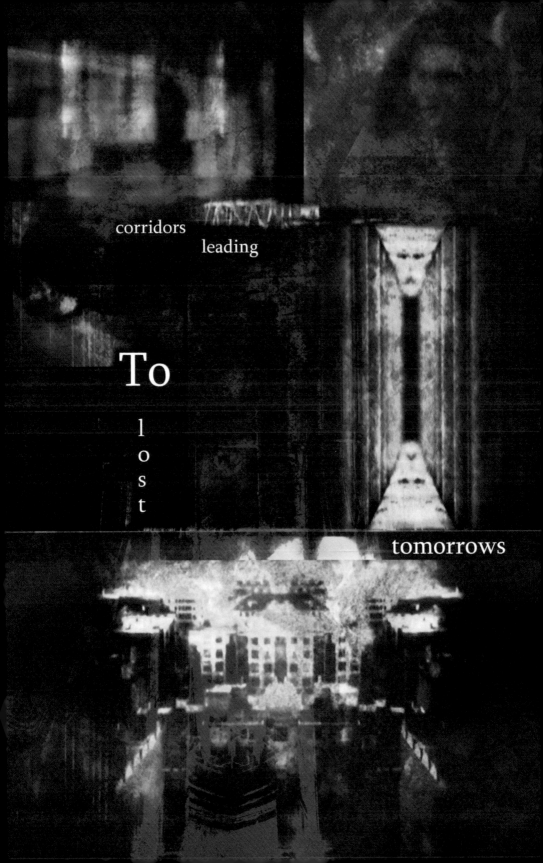

corridors

leading

To

l
o
s
t

tomorrows

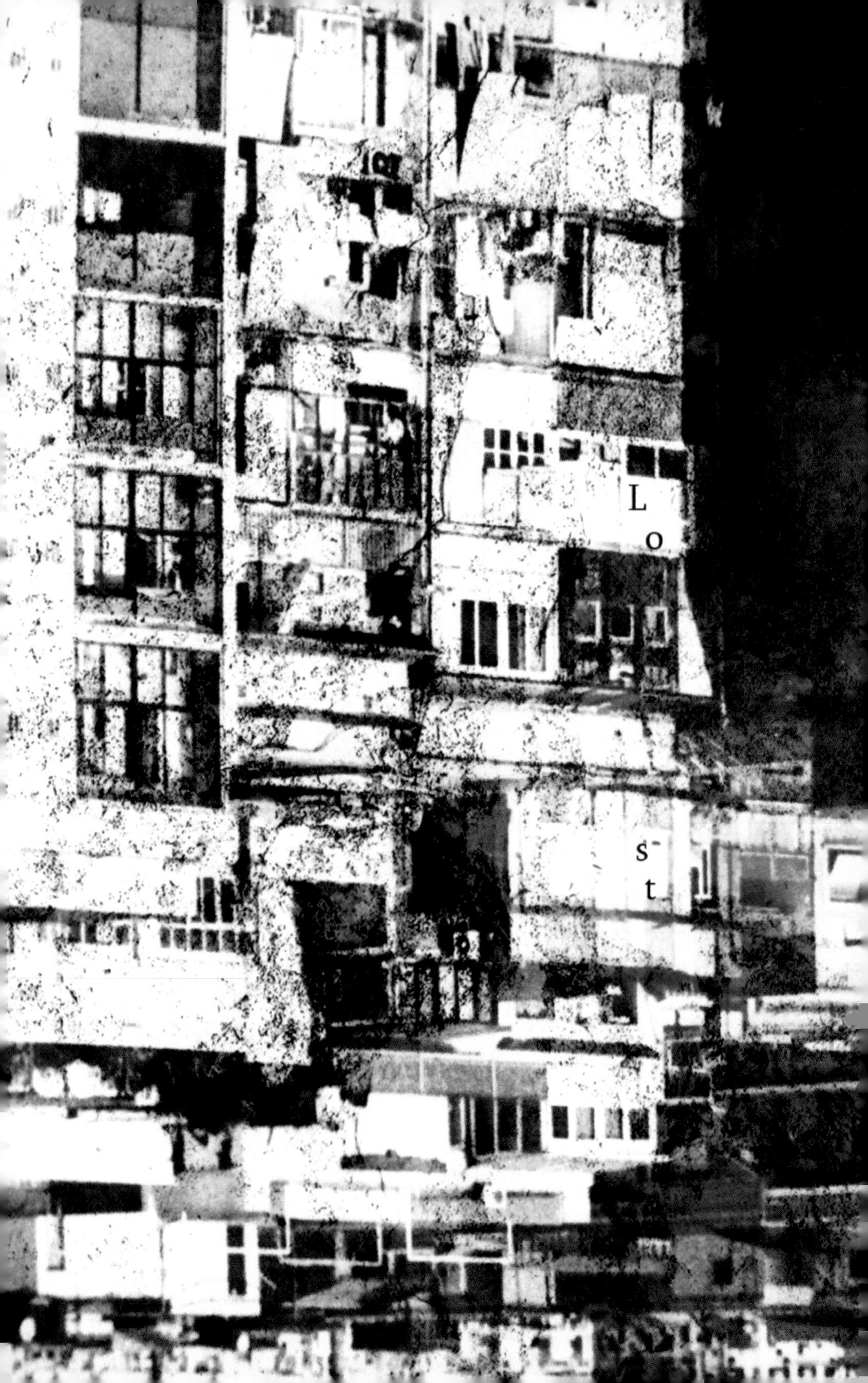
Lost

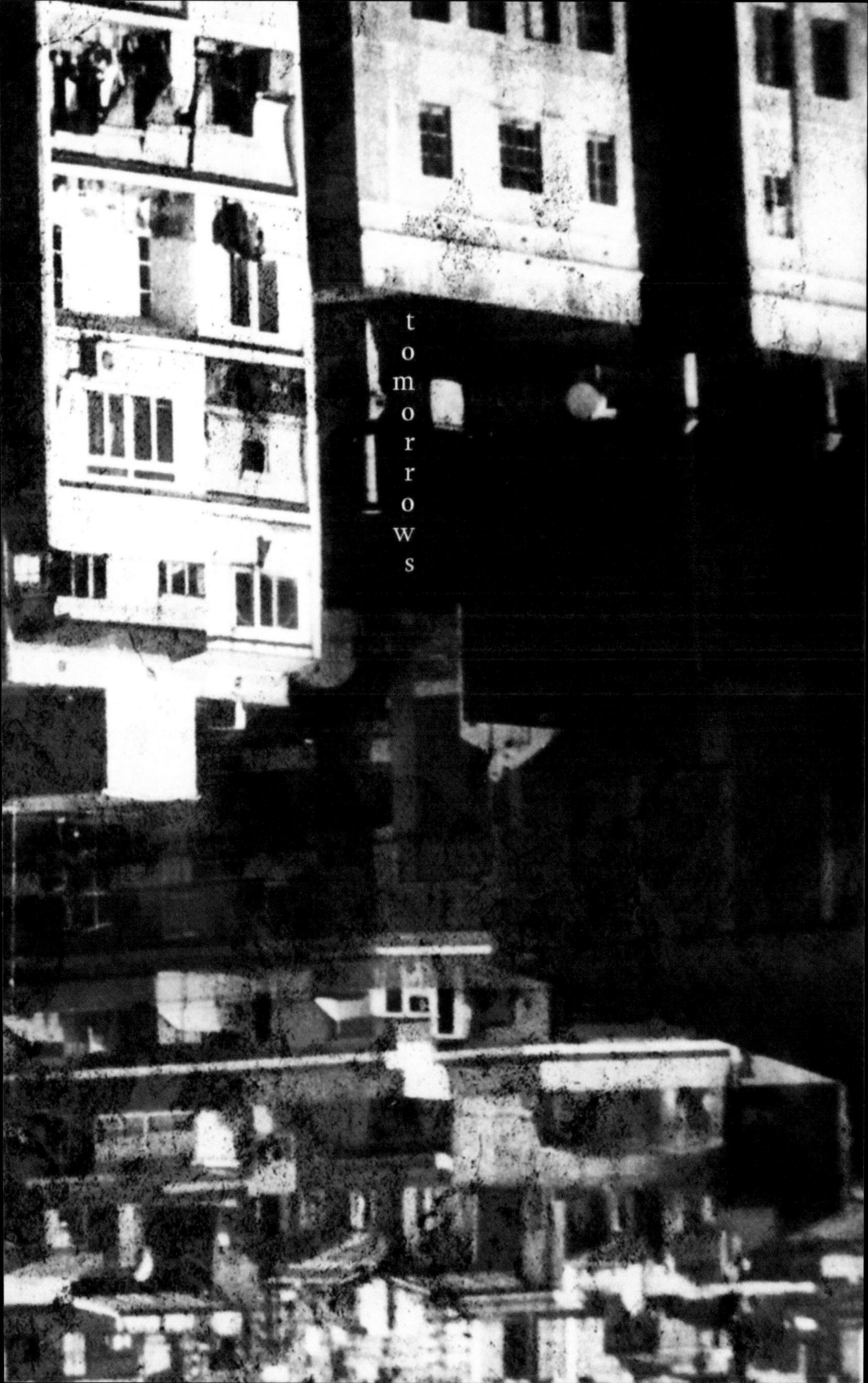
tomorrows

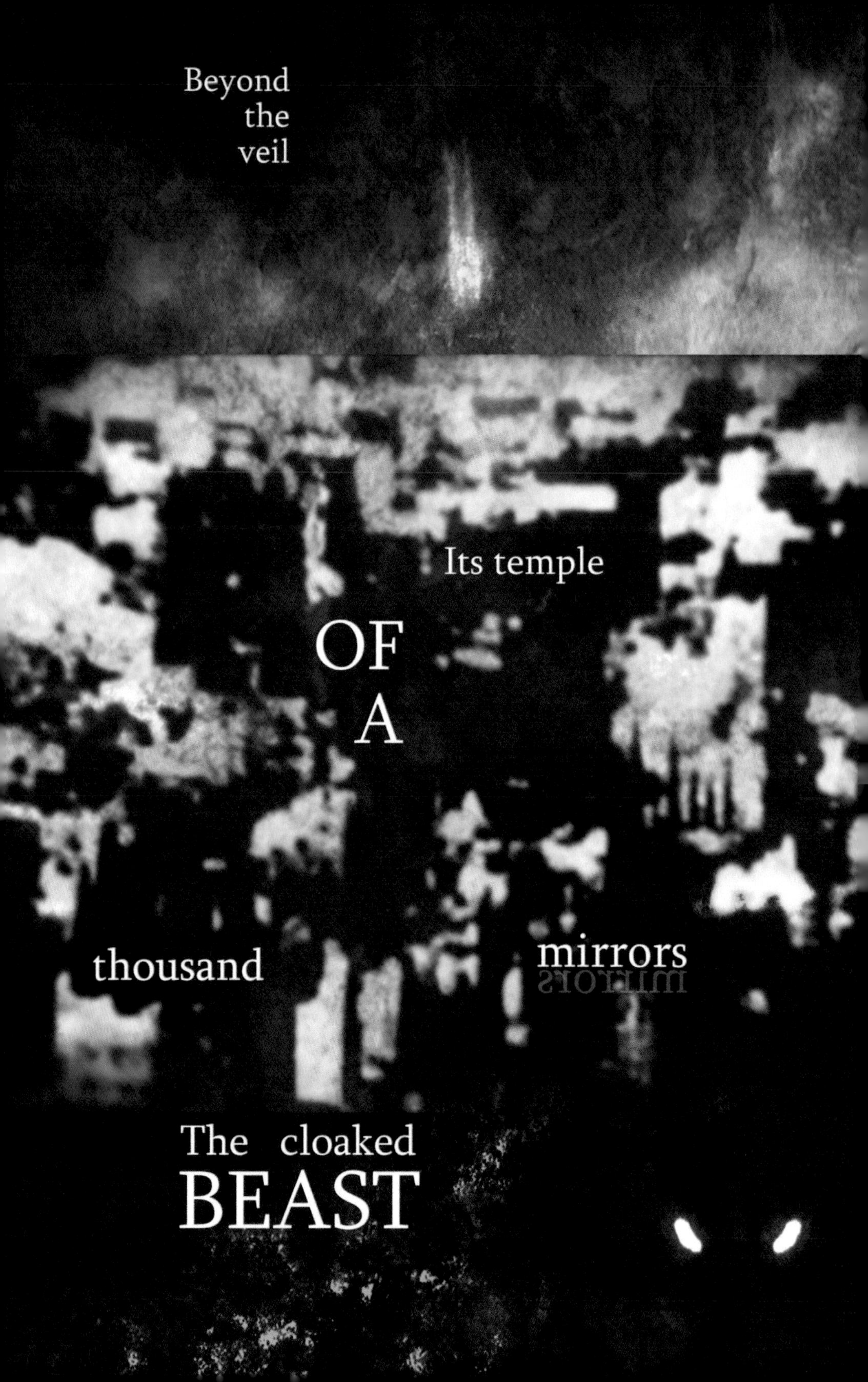
Beyond
the
veil
Its temple
OF
A
thousand
mirrors
The cloaked
BEAST

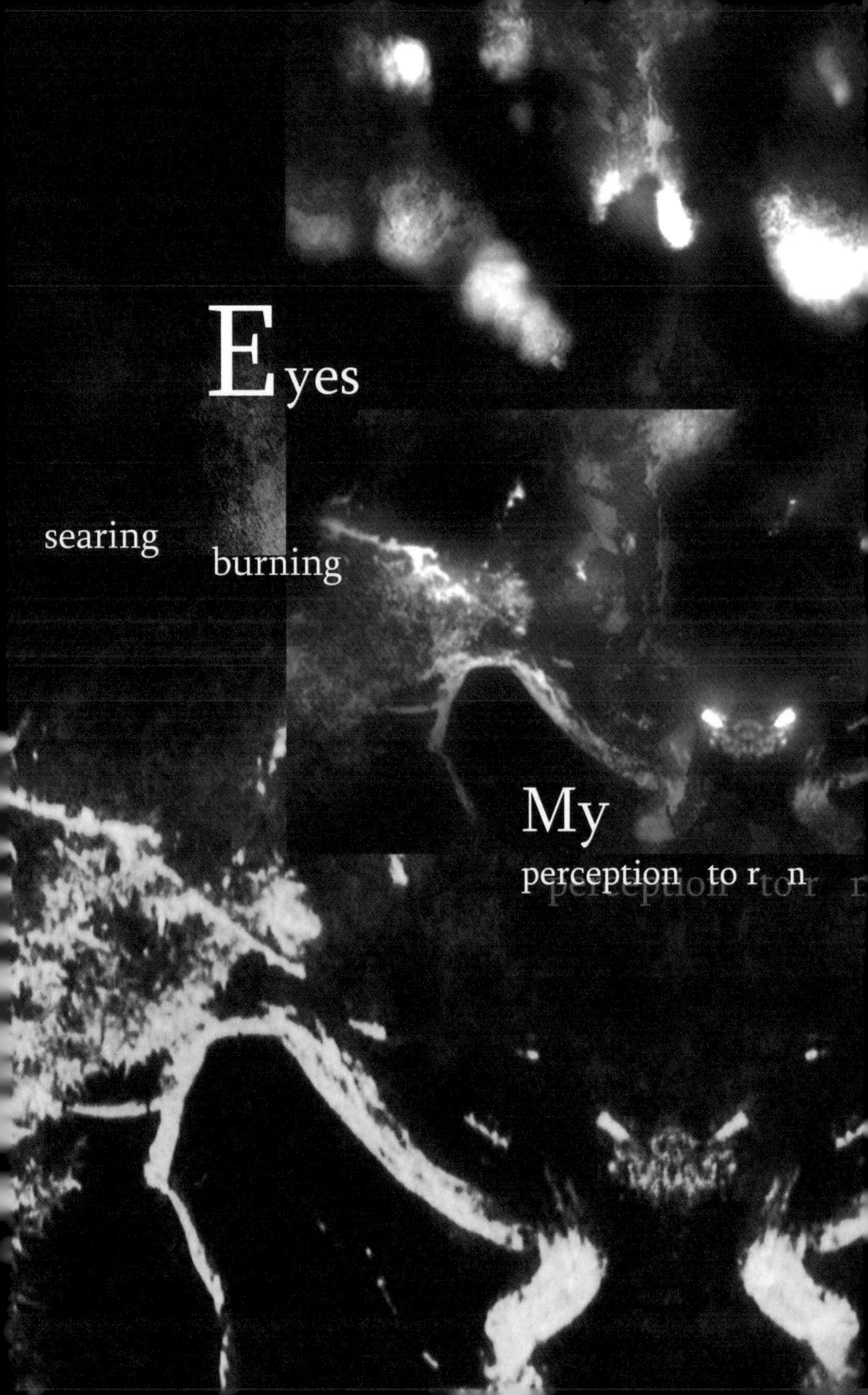
Eyes
searing
burning
My
perception to r n

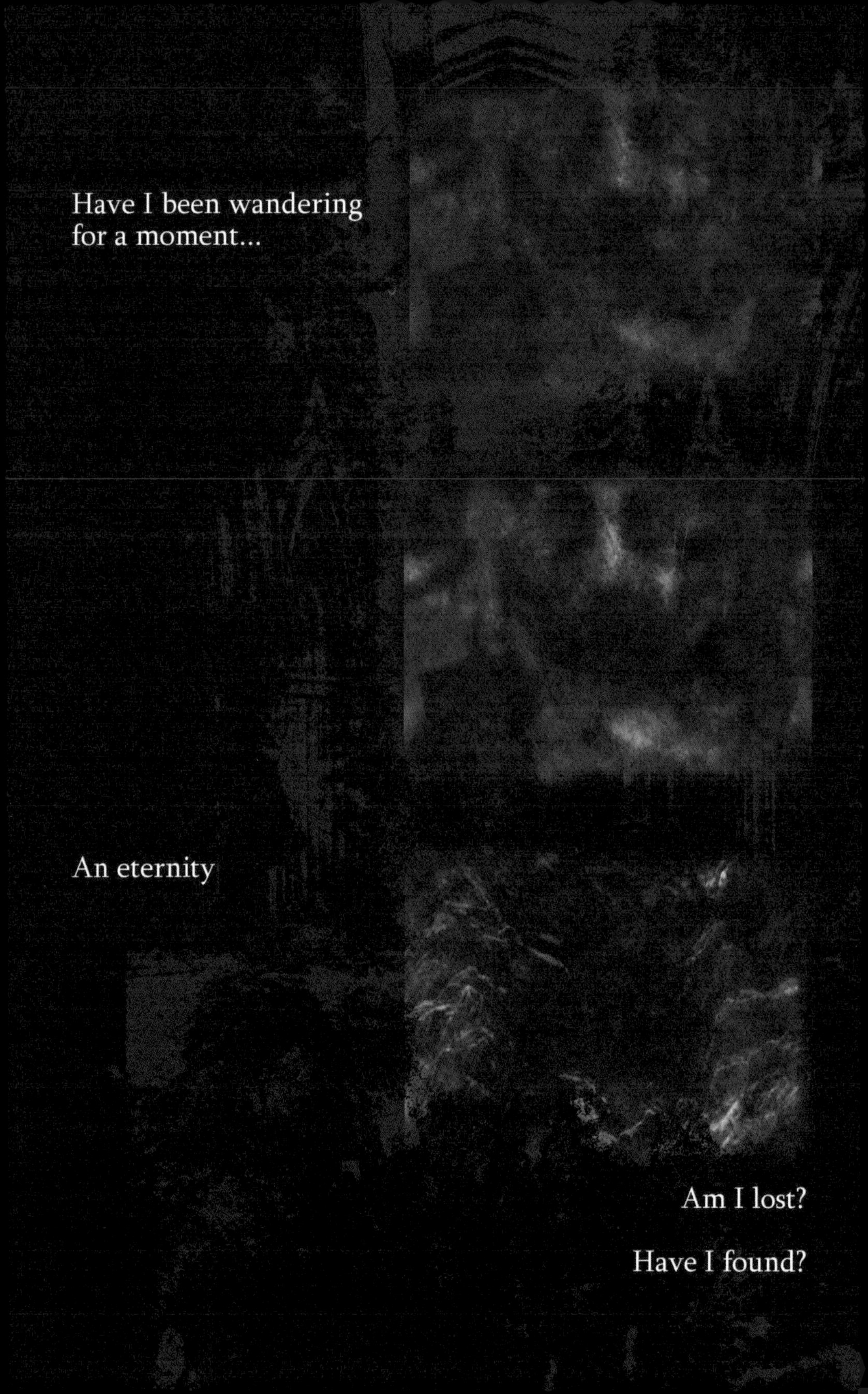

Have I been wandering
for a moment...

An eternity

Am I lost?

Have I found?

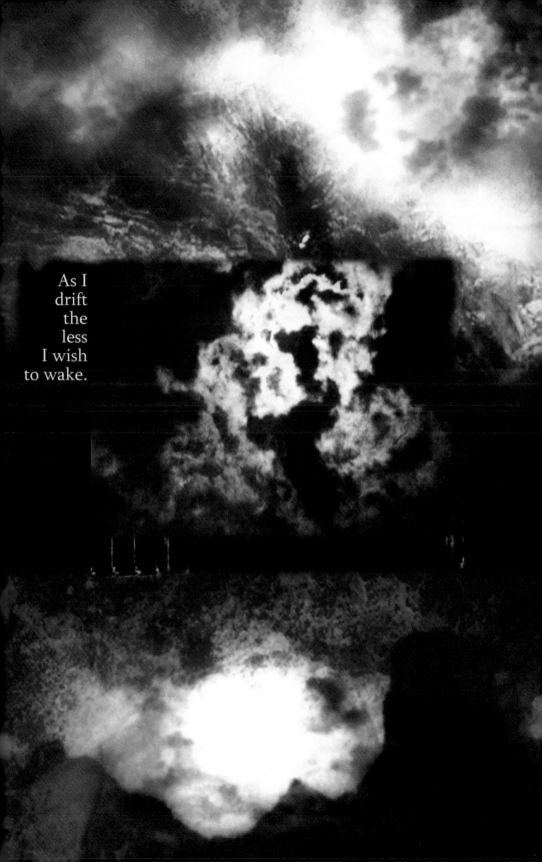

As I
drift
the
less
I wish
to wake.

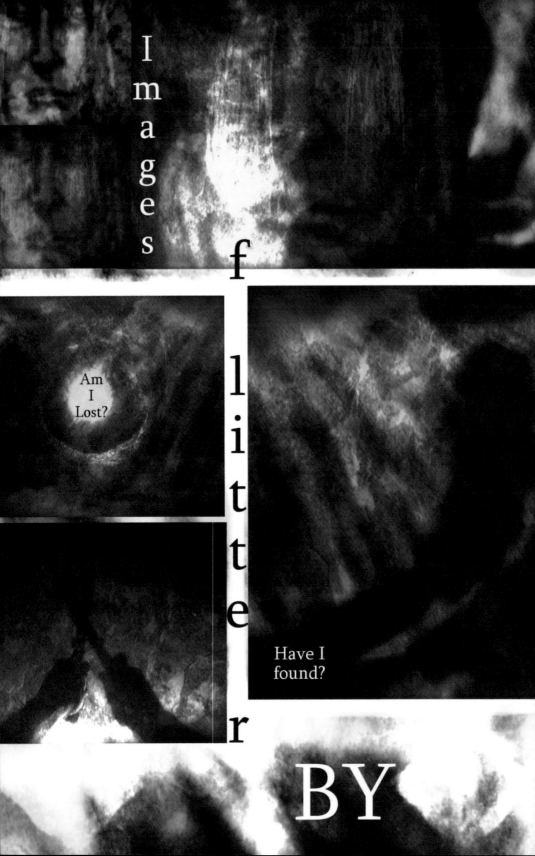

Images
f
litter

Am
I
Lost?

Have I
found?

BY

Am I
fool?

O
r
a
c
l
e
?

Beast

Images flitter by:
A face
Half-remembered,

familiar yet strange

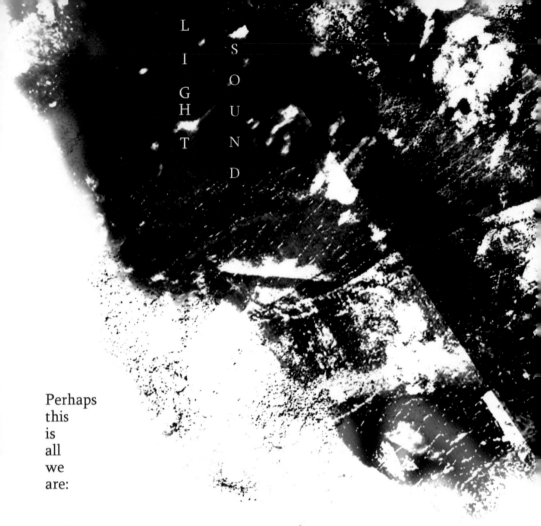

L
I
G
H
T

S
O
U
N
D

Perhaps
this
is
all
we
are:

Light
and
Sound,

Perhaps...

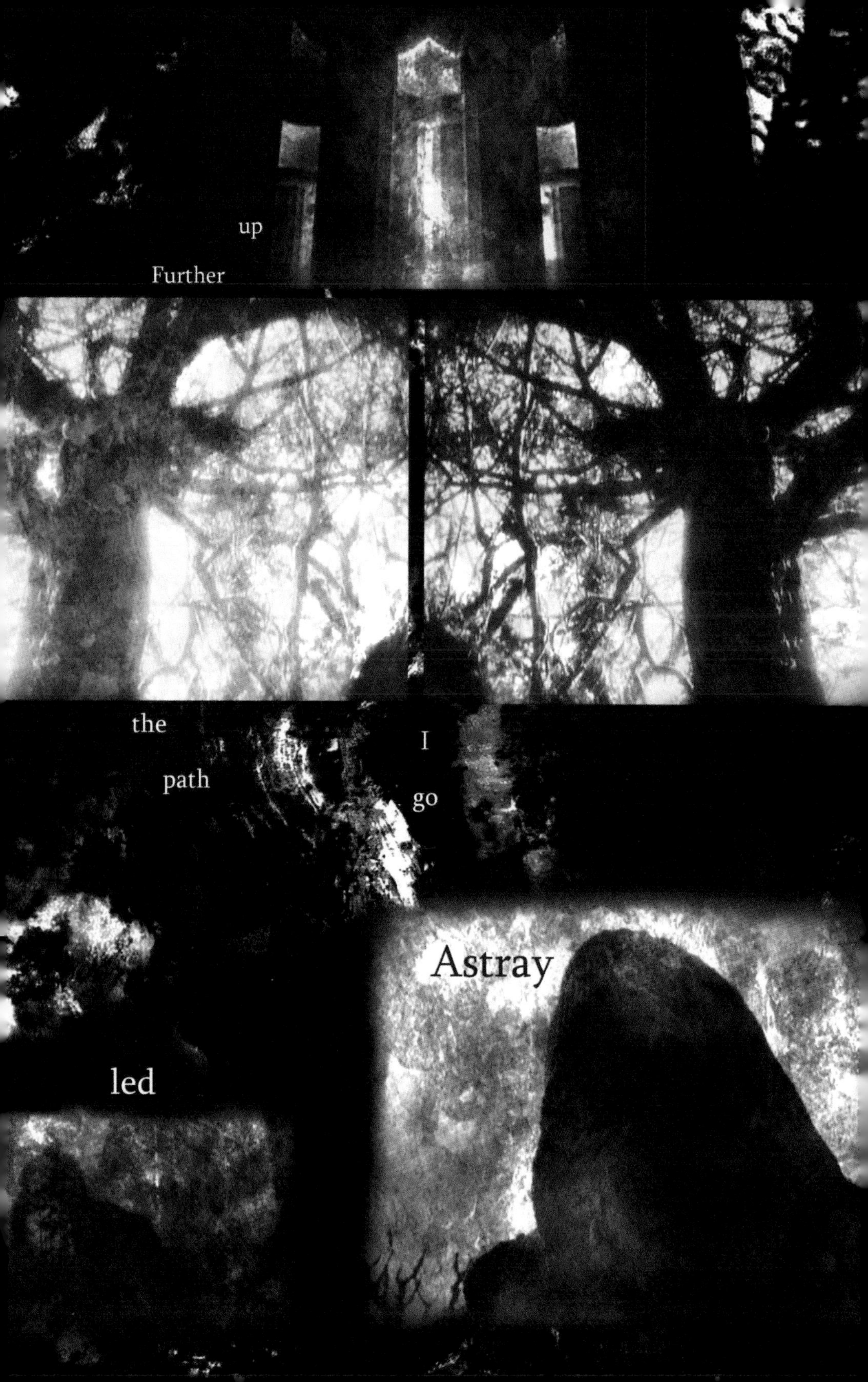
up
Further
the
I
path
go
Astray
led

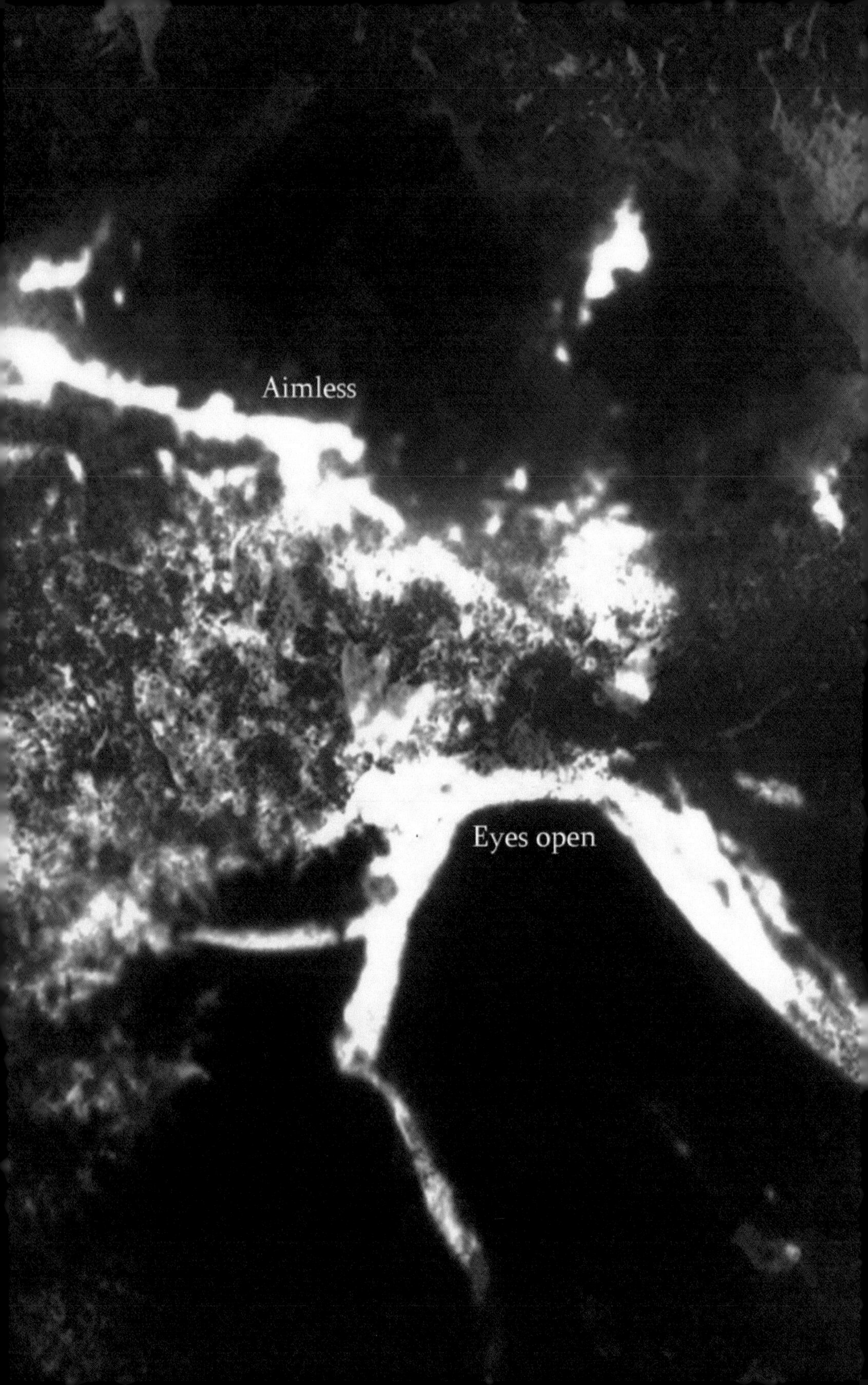
Aimless
Eyes open

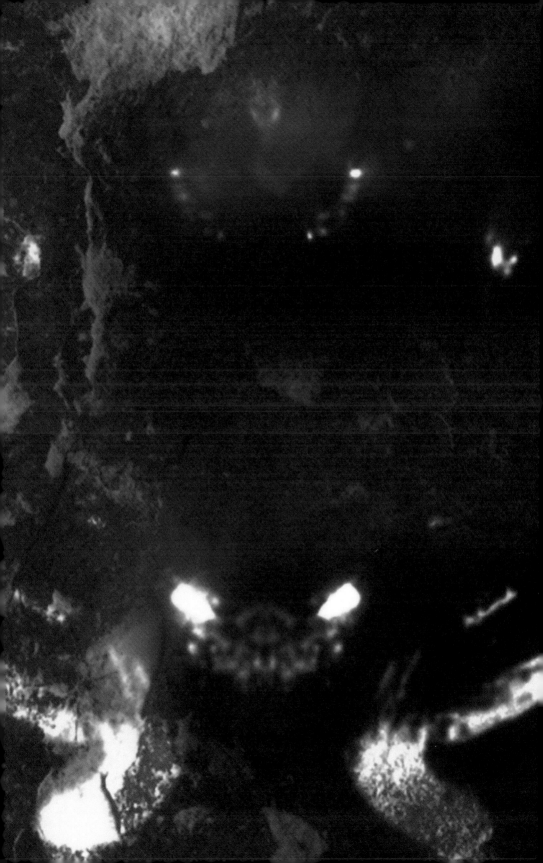

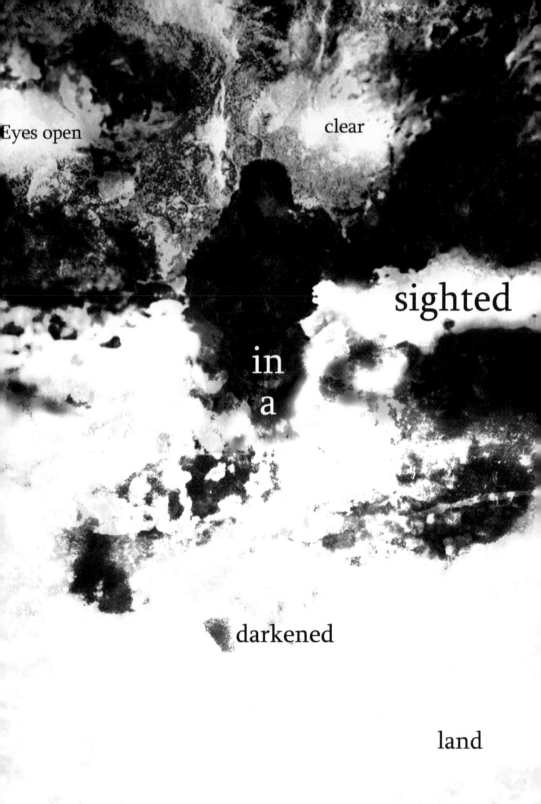

Eyes open

clear

sighted

in

a

darkened

land

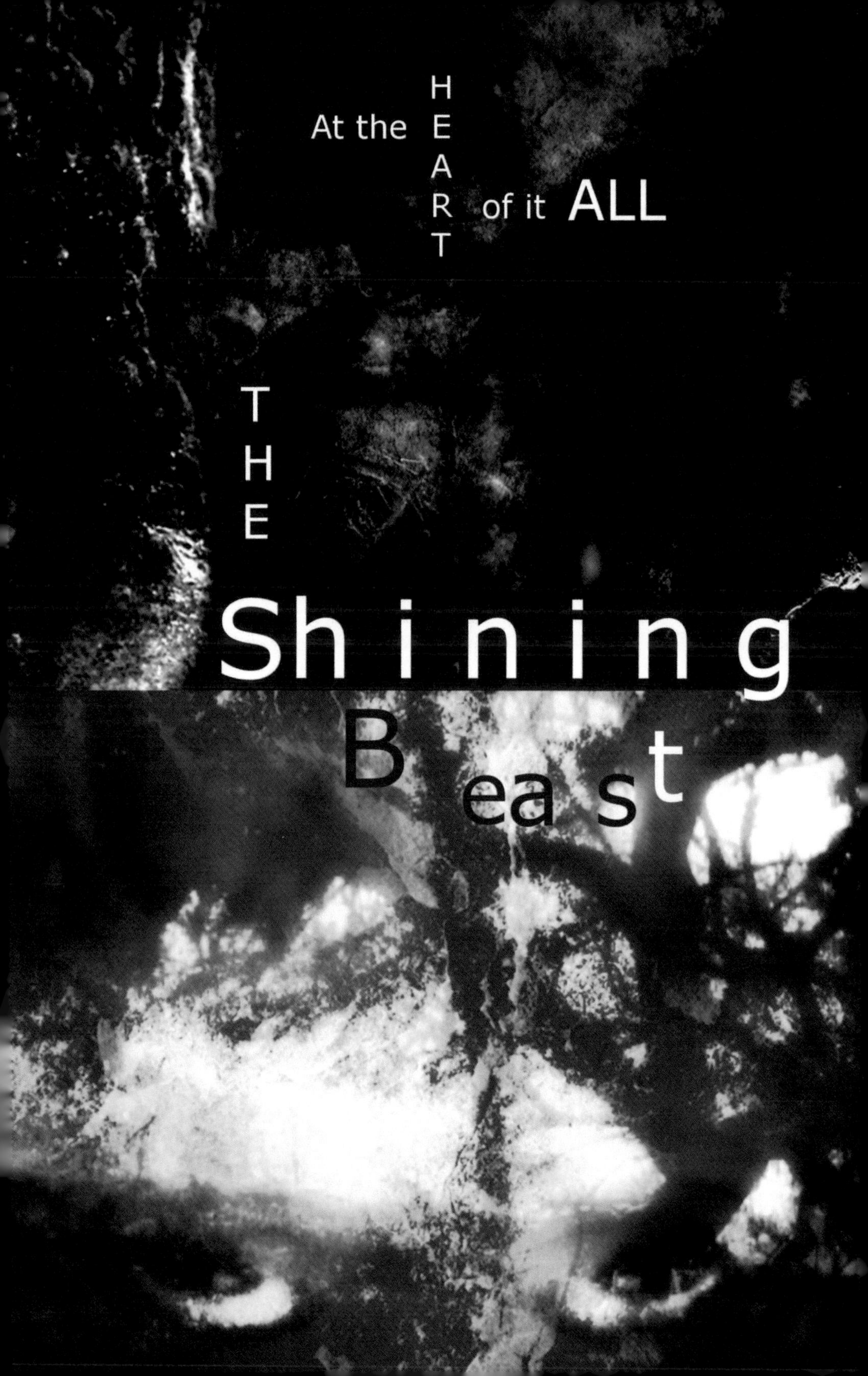
At the HEART of it ALL
THE
Shining
Beast

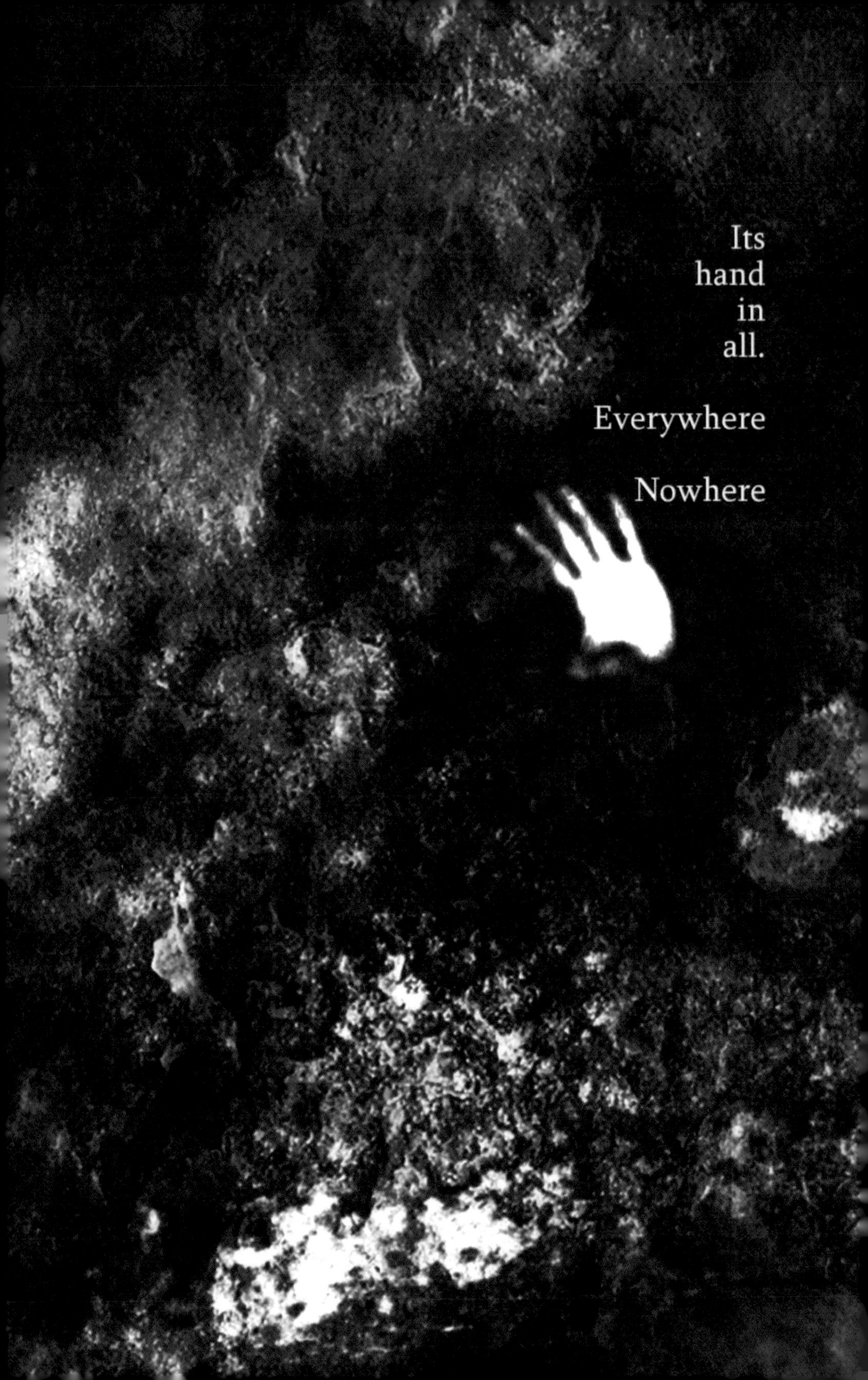

Its
hand
in
all.

Everywhere

Nowhere

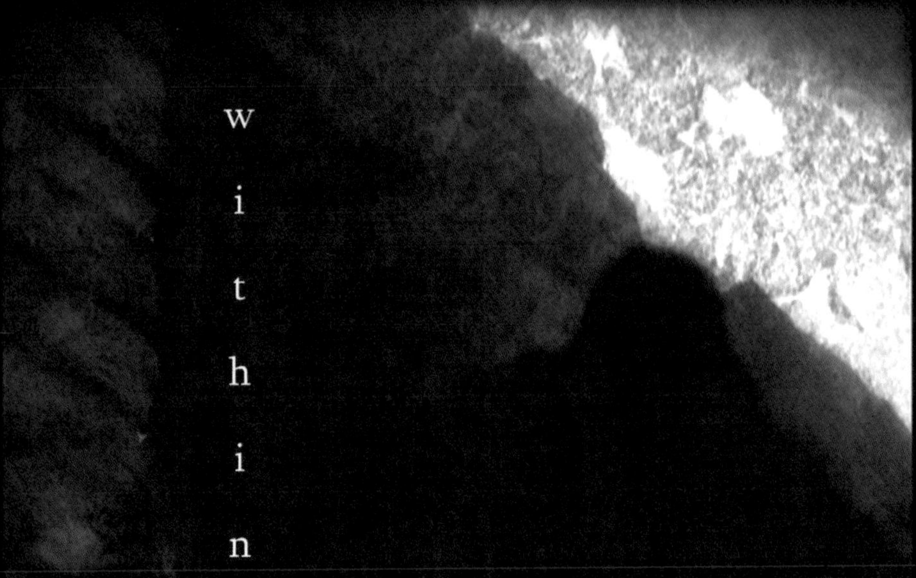

within

without

relentless

un blinking

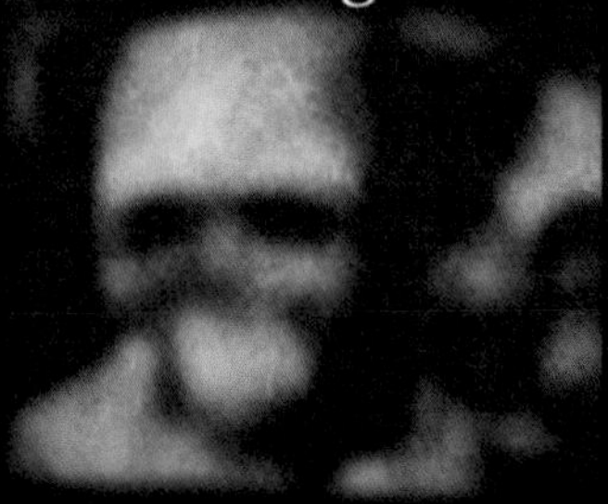

Soothing

Battering

Renewing

Destroying

B
r
o
k
e
n

j
a
d
e
d

Relentless,

un blinking.

l
o
s
t

A d   r i   f t

A scab   i n

the
psyche.   e.

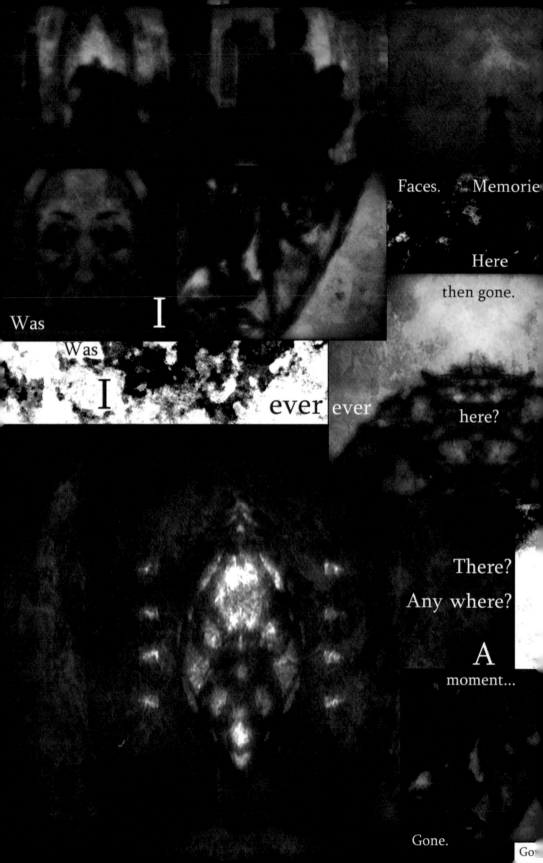

Faces.   Memorie

Here

then gone.

Was   I

Was

I

ever ever

here?

There?

Any where?

A

moment...

Gone.

Go

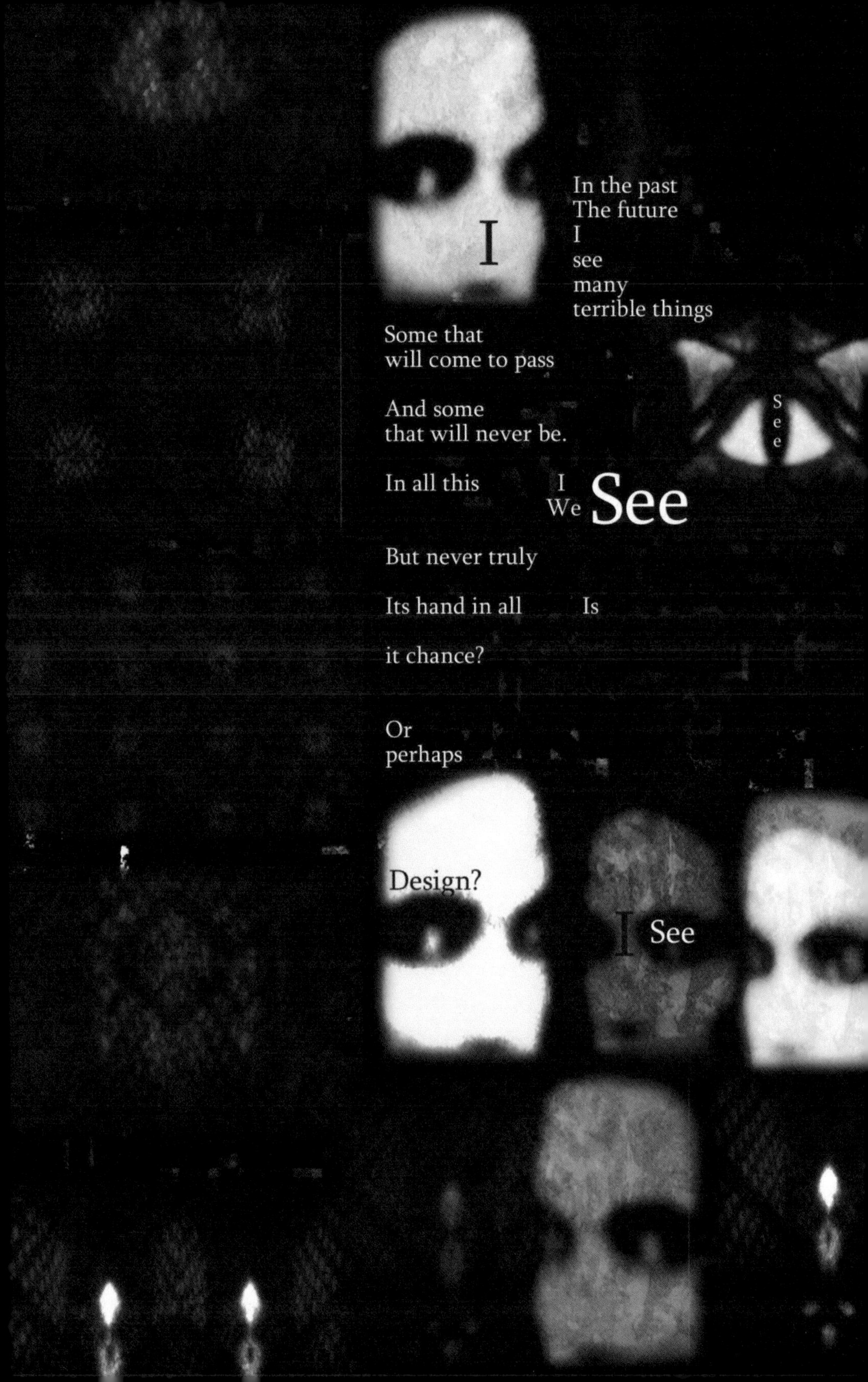
In the past
The future
I
see
many
terrible things
I
Some that
will come to pass
And some
that will never be.
See
In all this
I
We
See
But never truly
Its hand in all
Is
it chance?
Or
perhaps
Design?
I
See

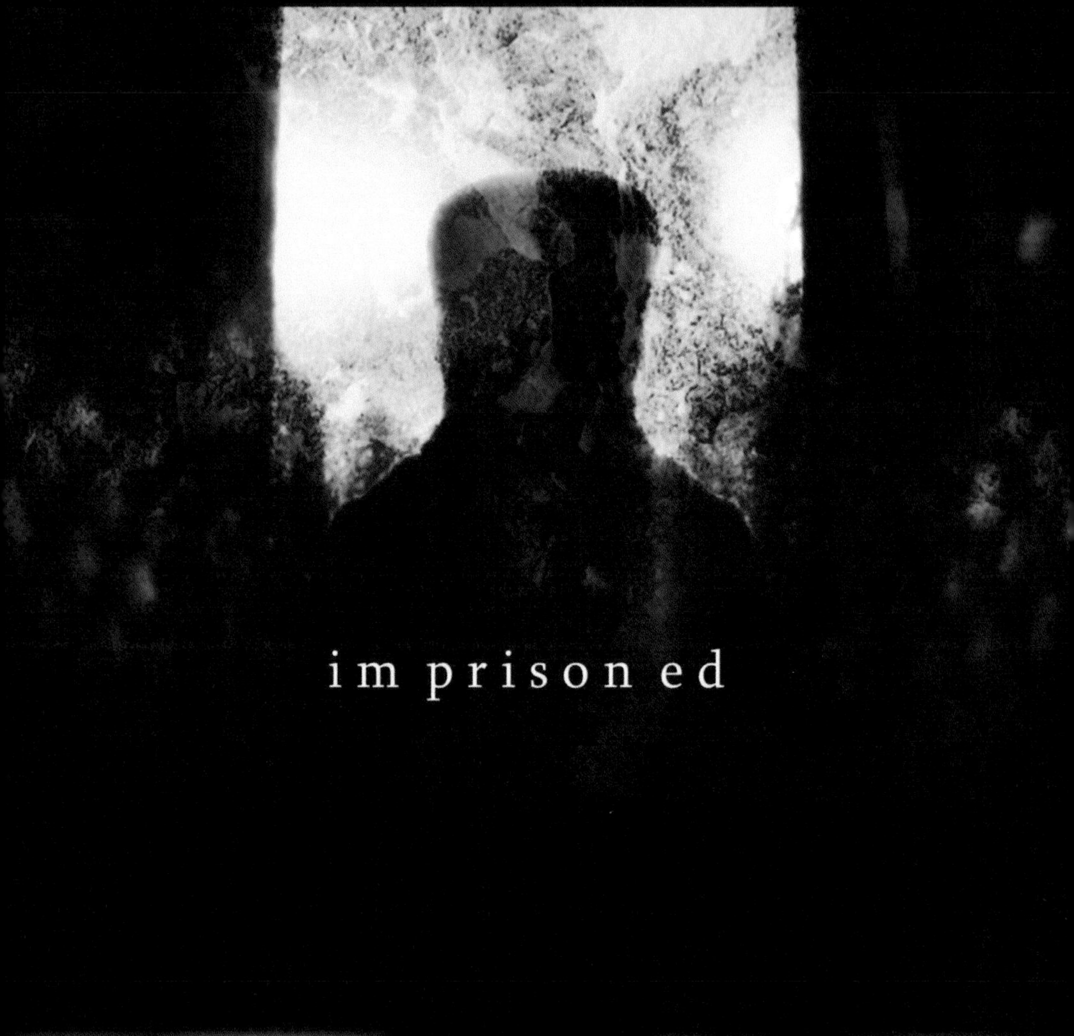

im prison ed

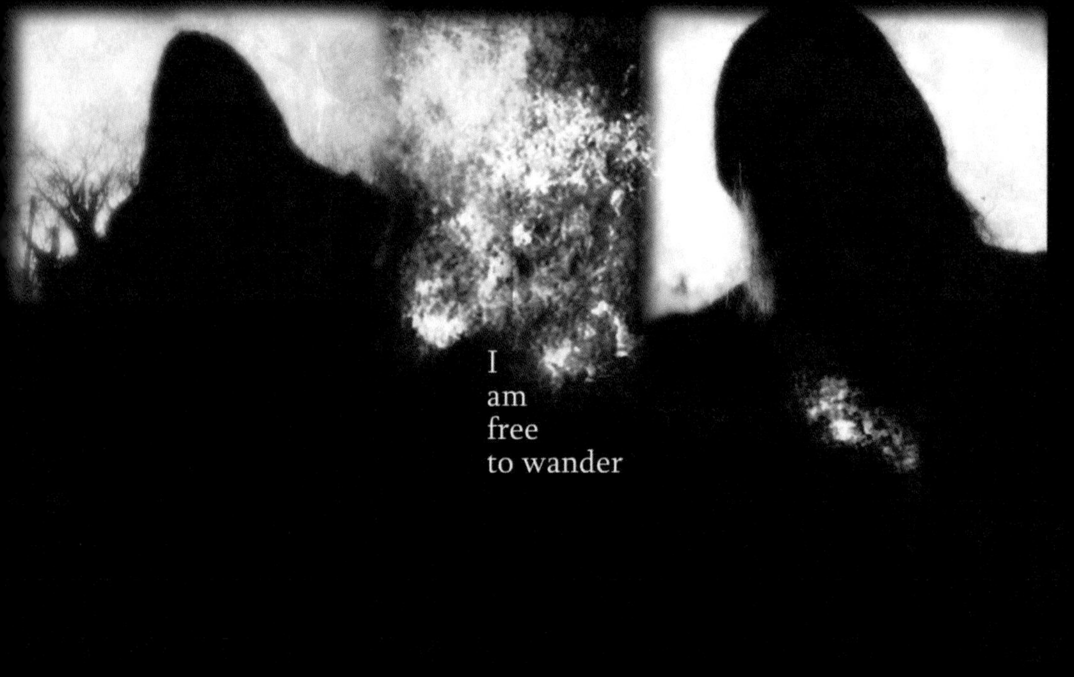

I
am
free
to wander

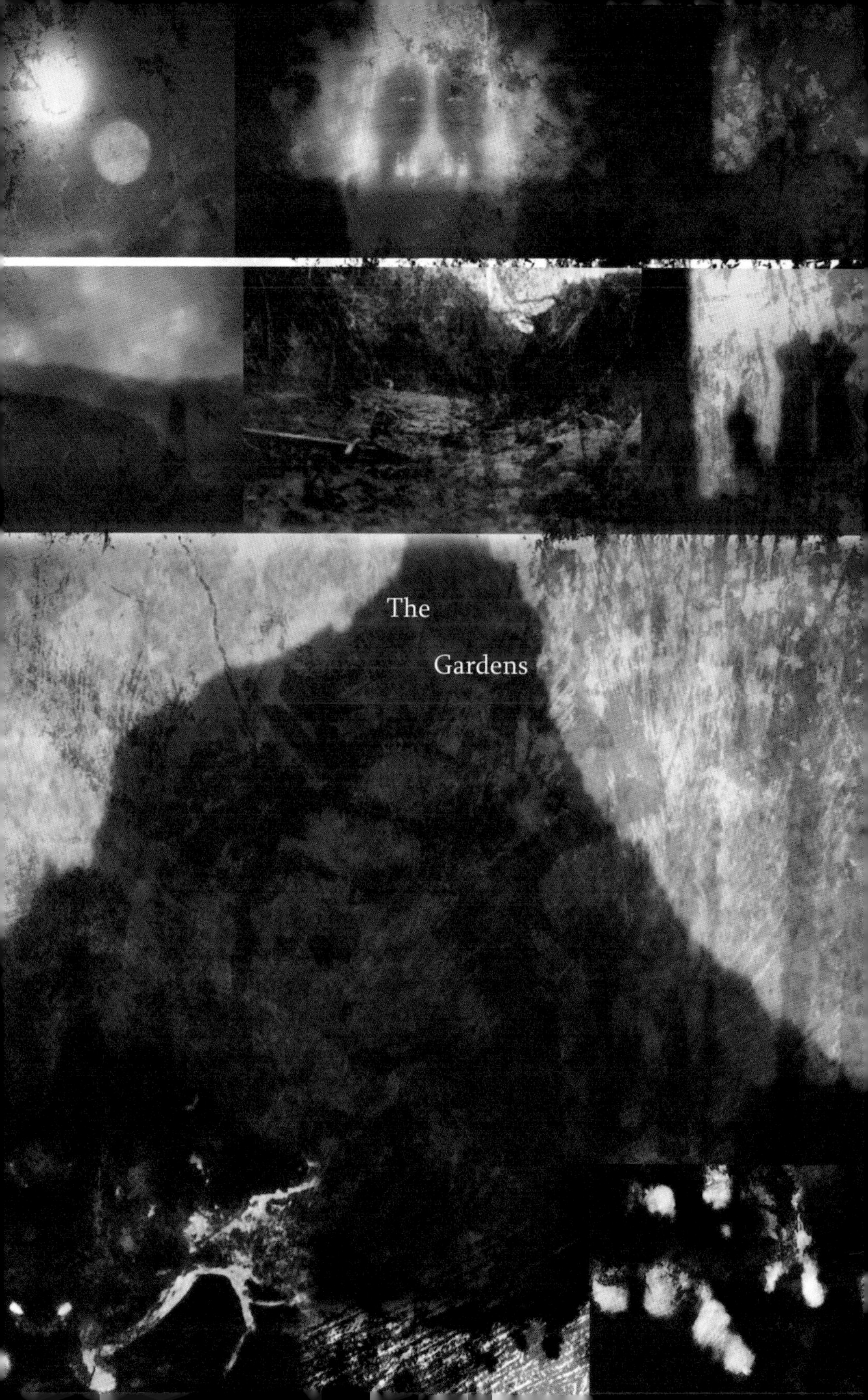
The
Gardens

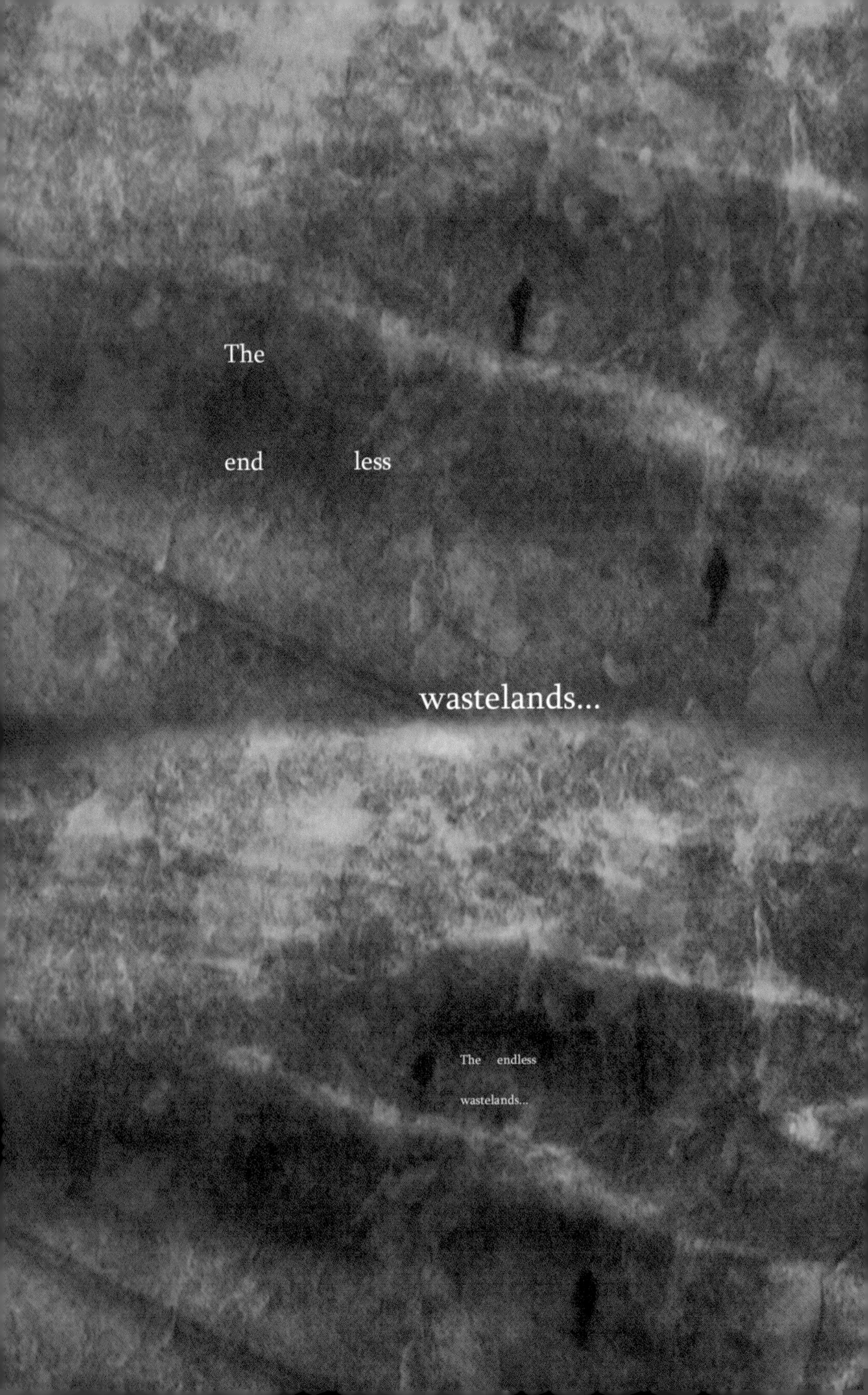
The
end less
wastelands...
The endless
wastelands...

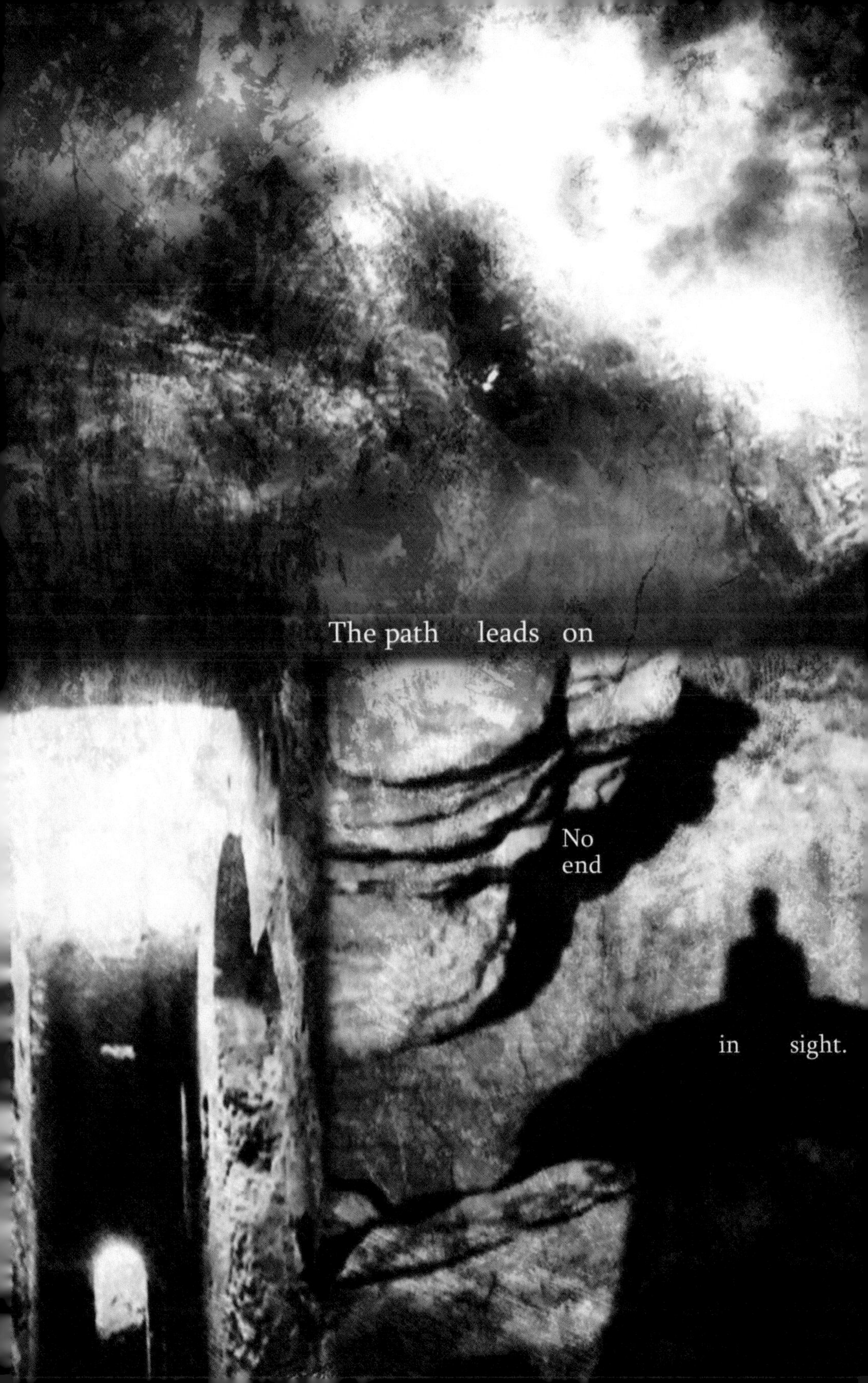

The path leads on

No
end

in sight.

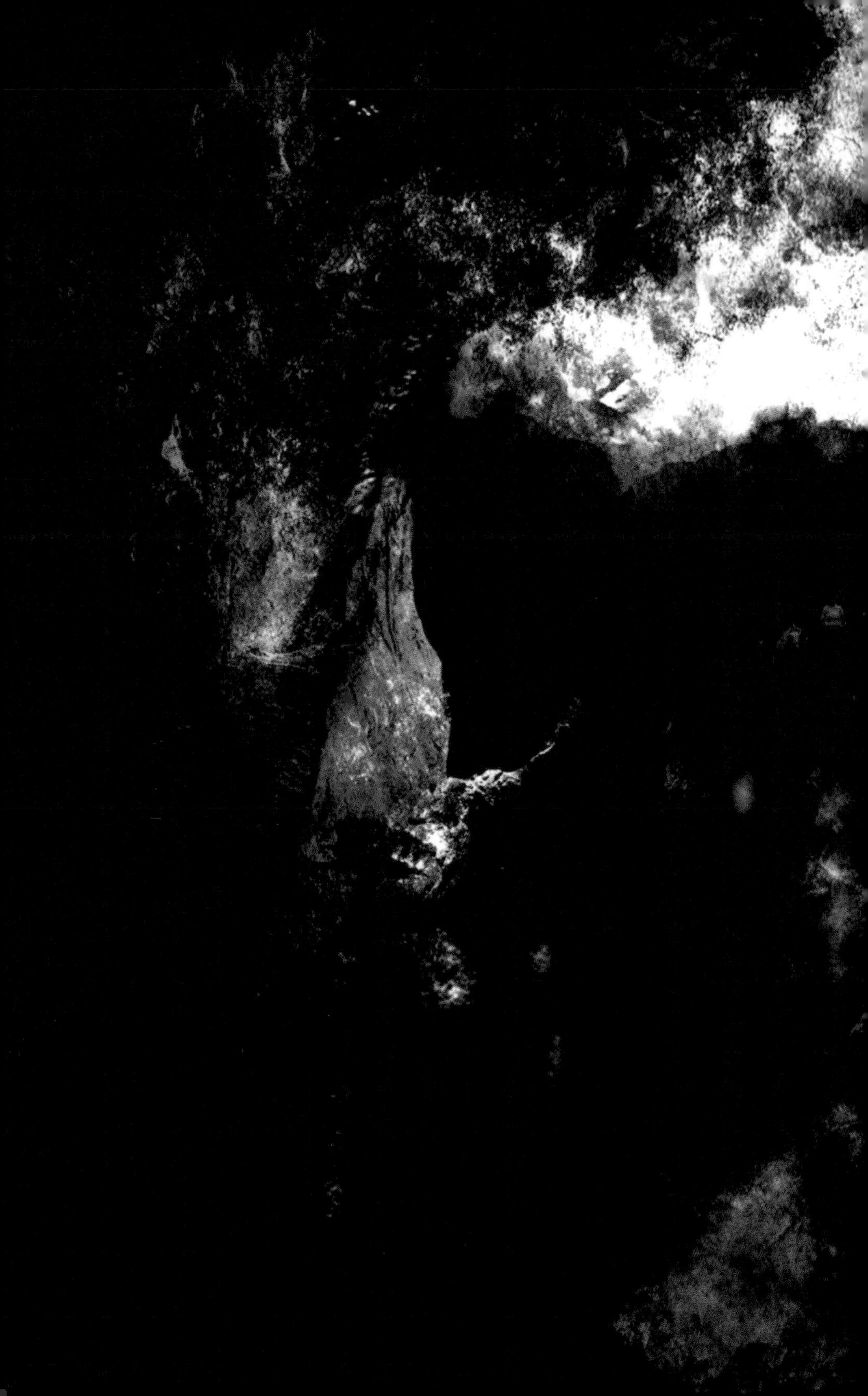

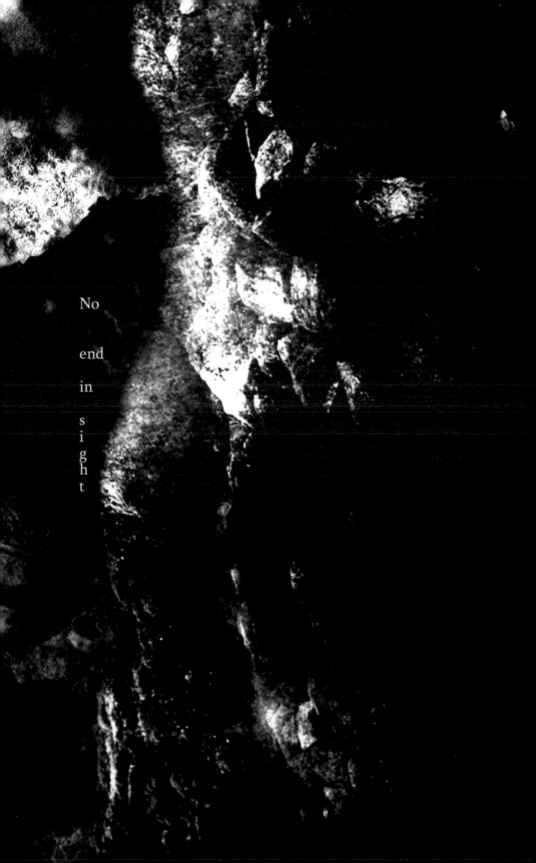

No
end
in
s
i
g
h
t

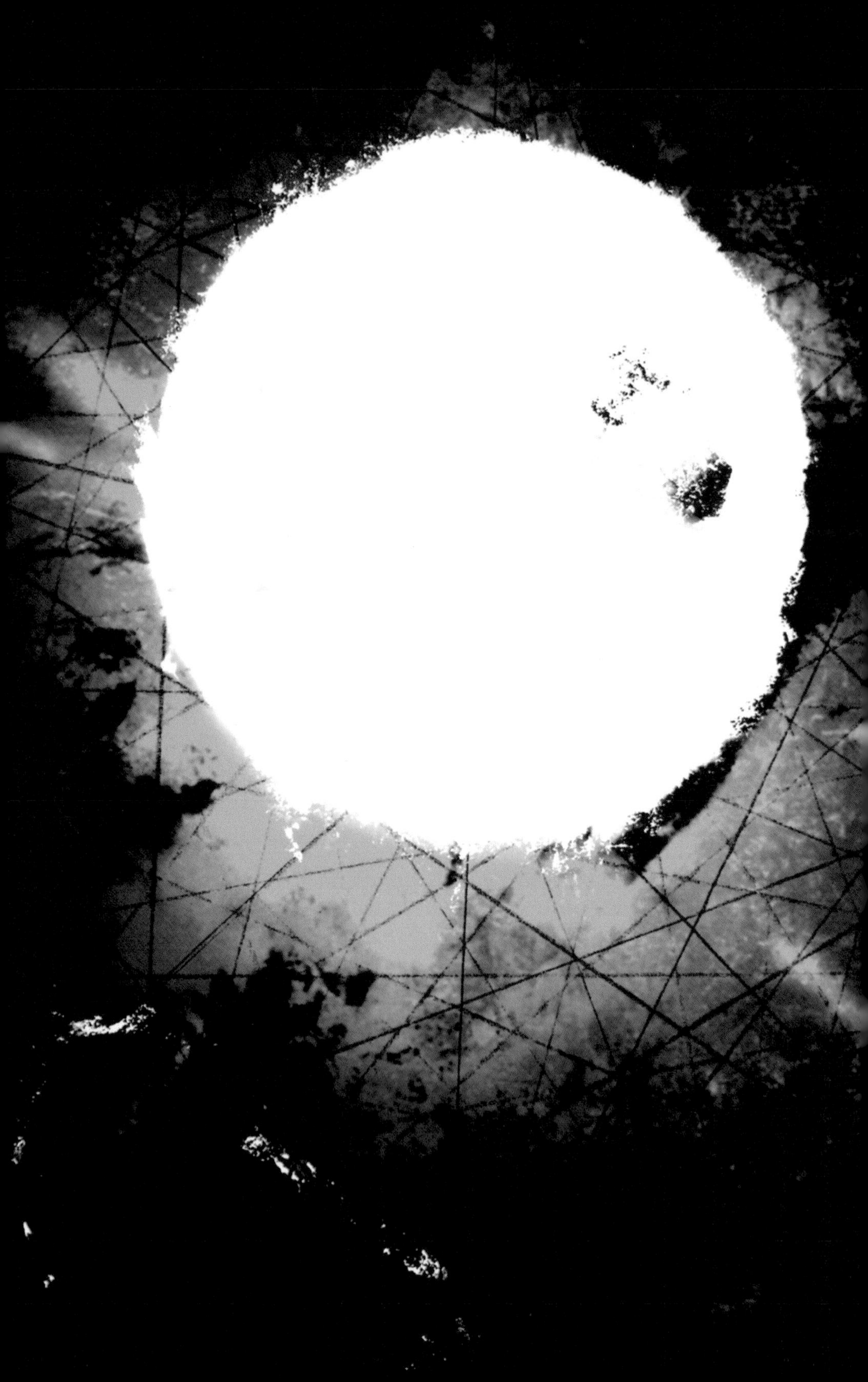

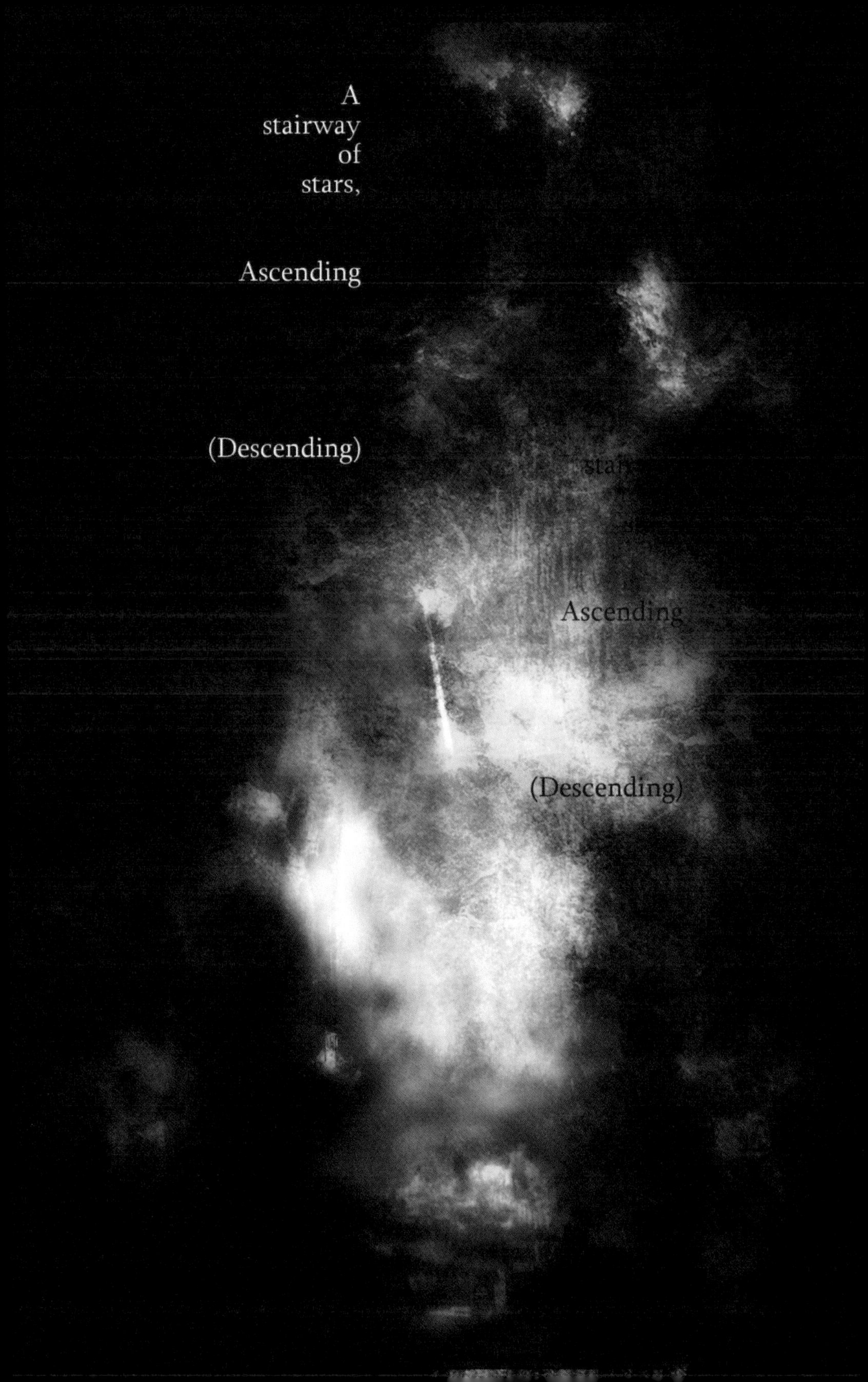
A
stairway
of
stars,
Ascending
(Descending)
Ascending
(Descending)

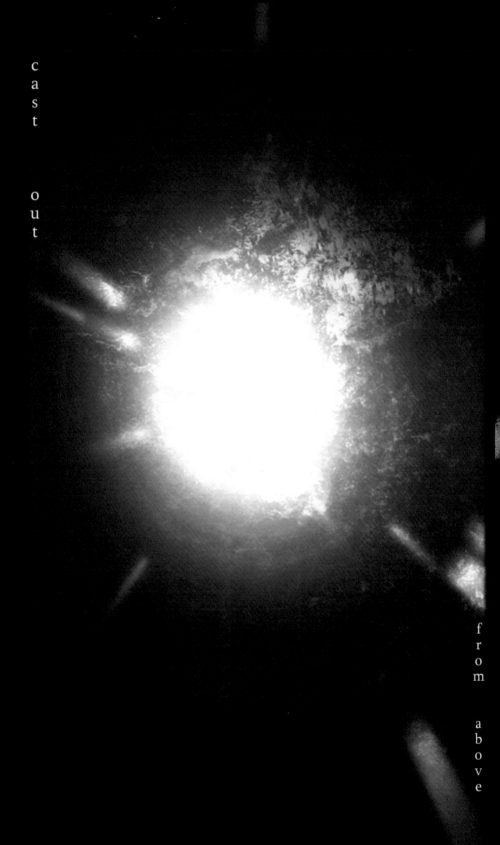

cast

out

from

above

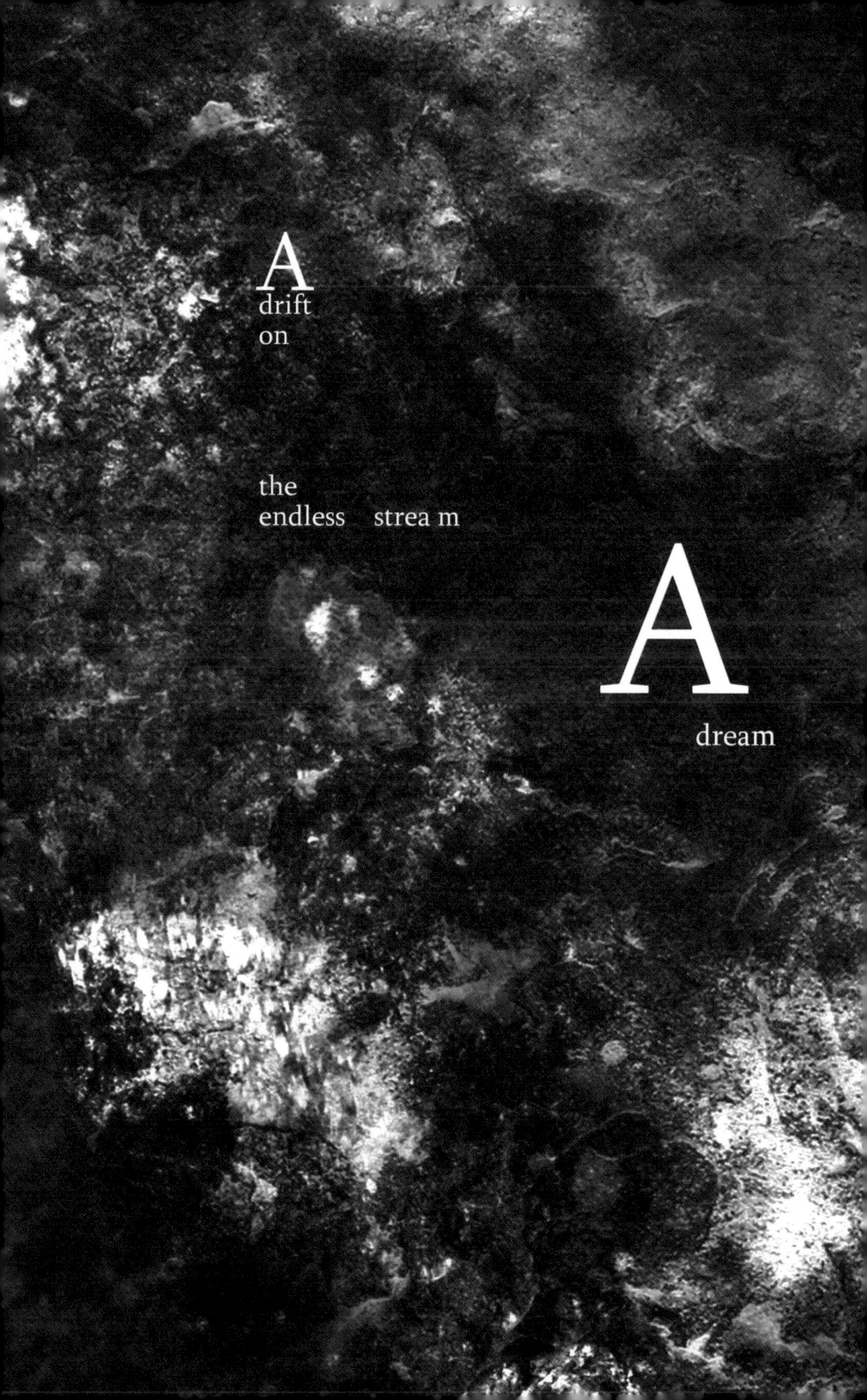

A
drift
on

the
endless strea m

A

dream

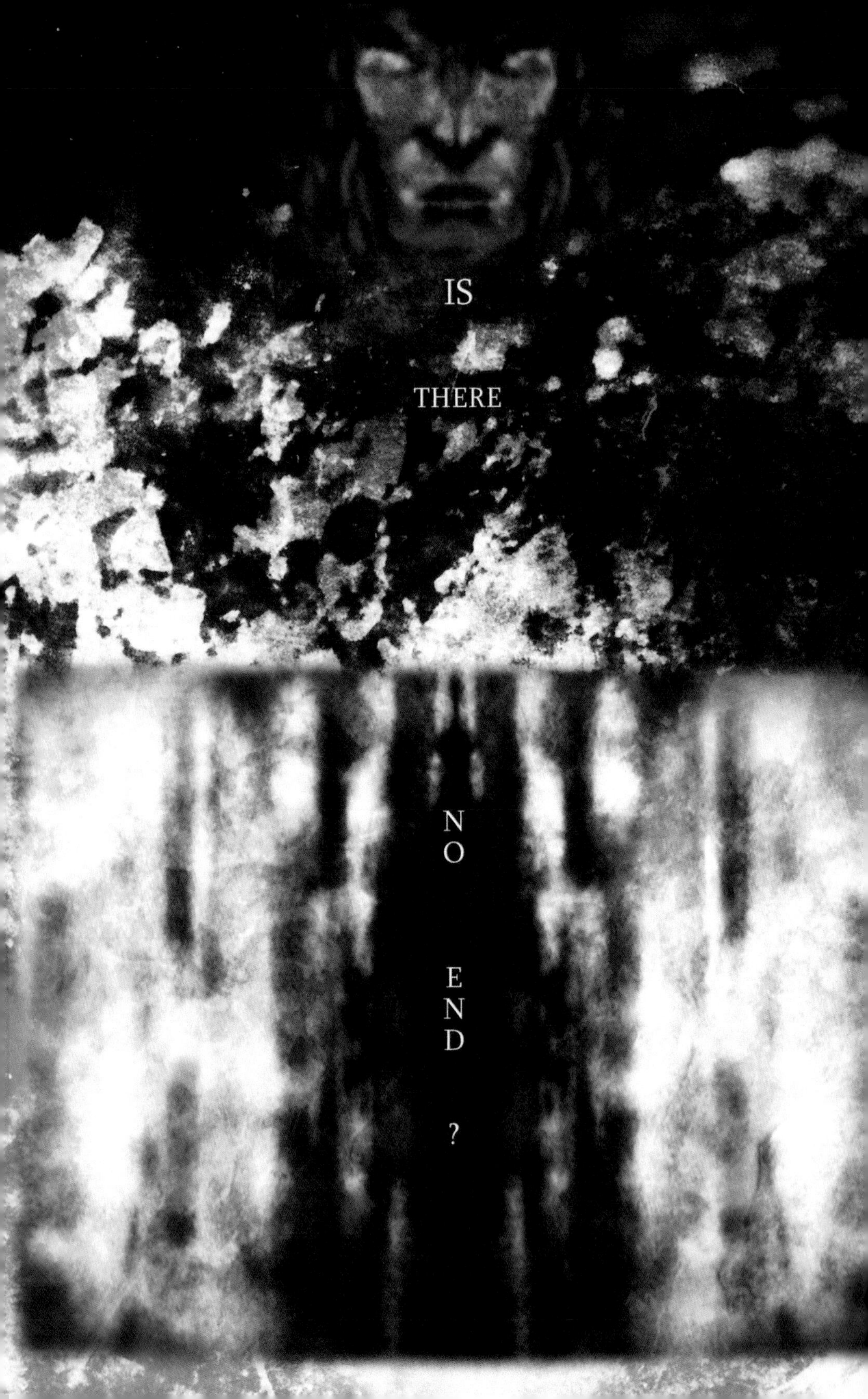
IS
THERE
NO
END
?

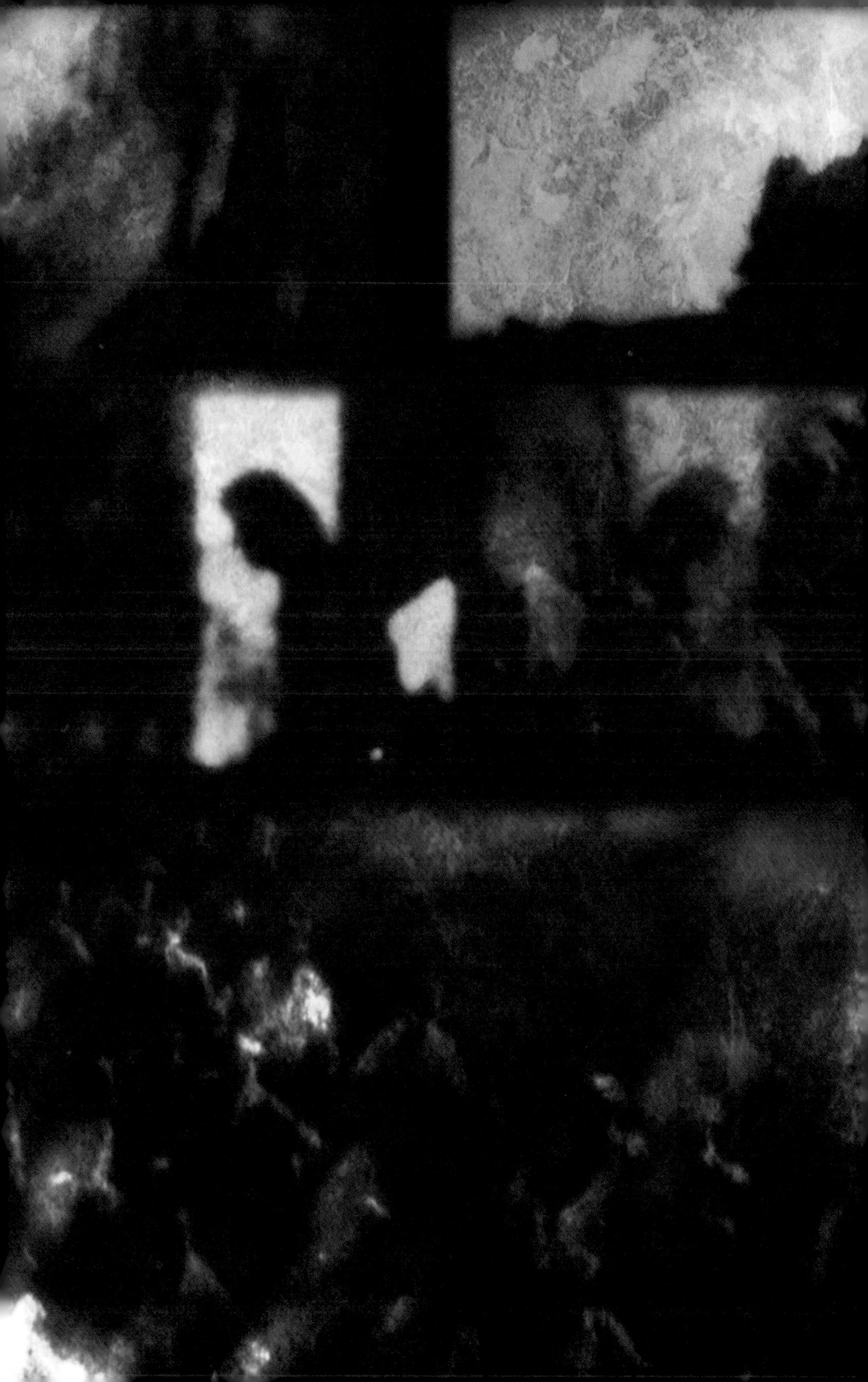

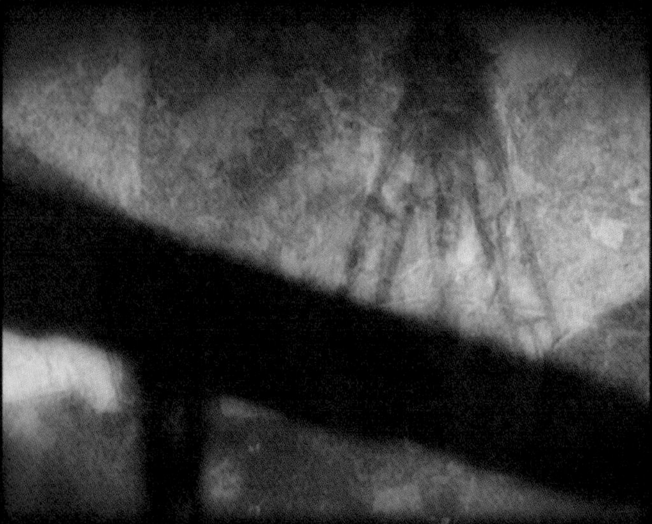

I see
THE

F
A
L
L

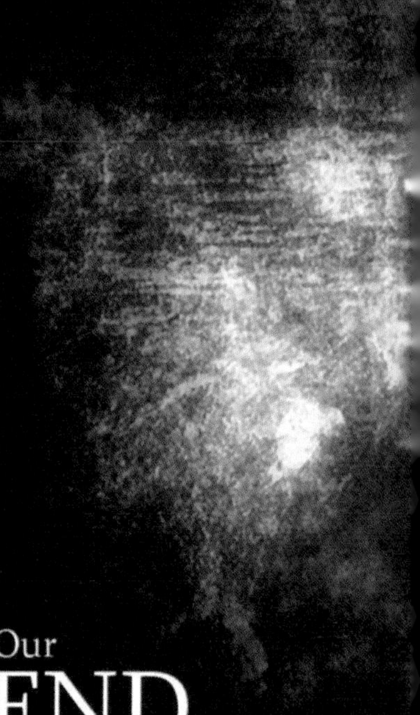

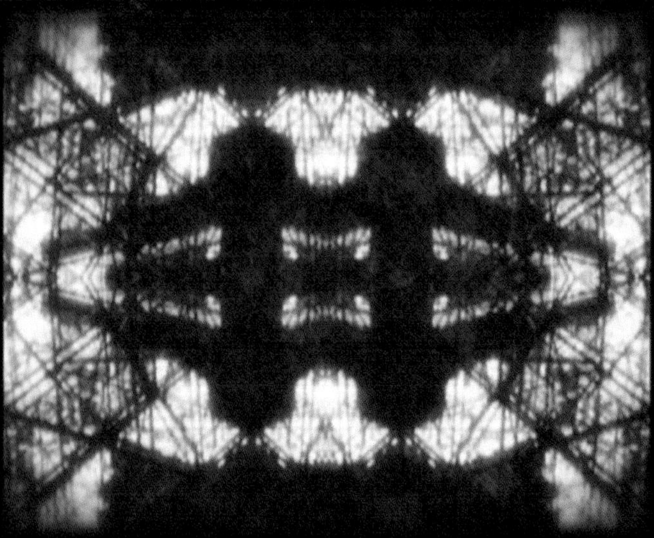

Our
END

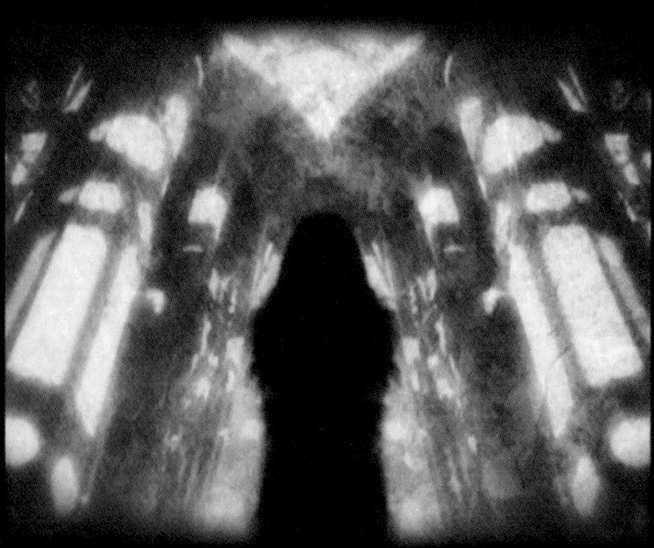

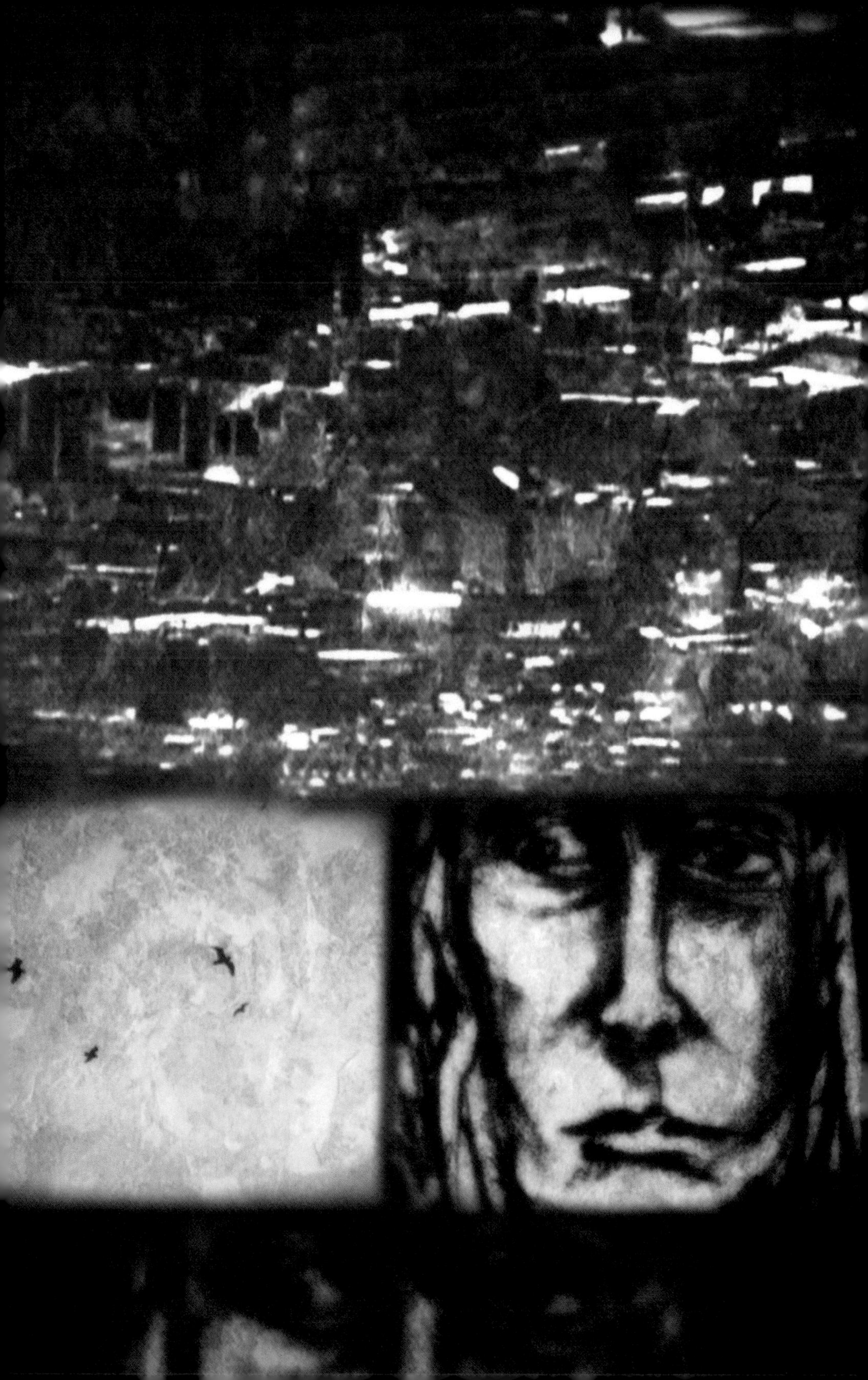

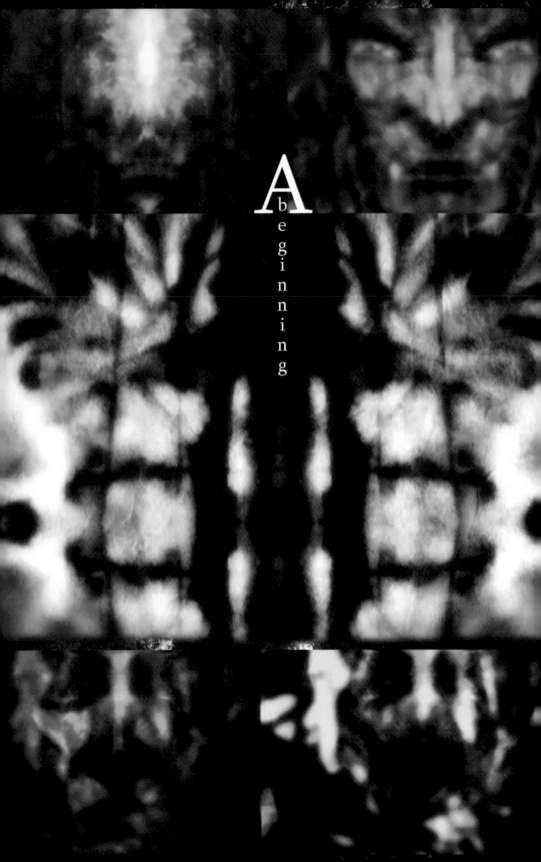

A
beginning

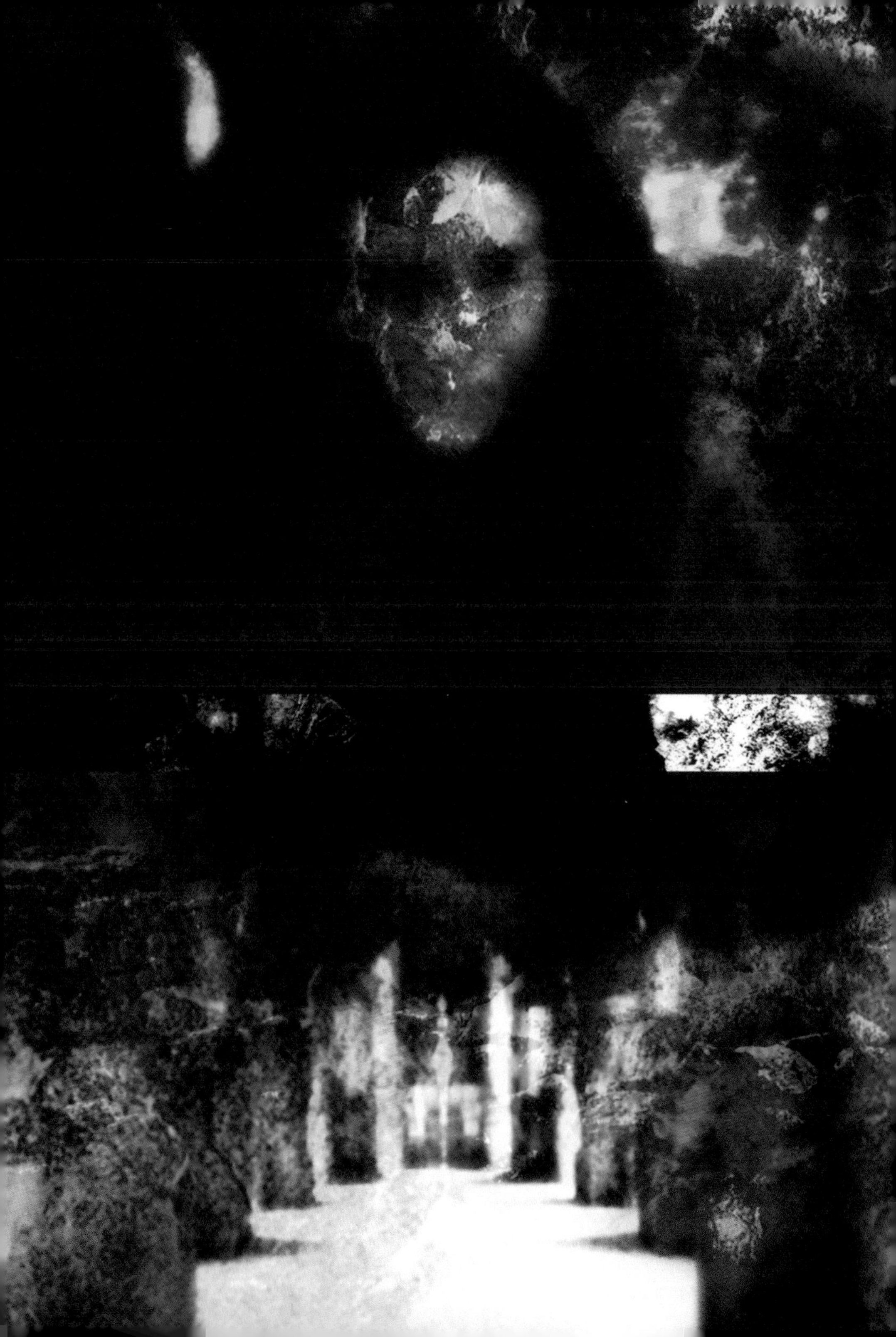

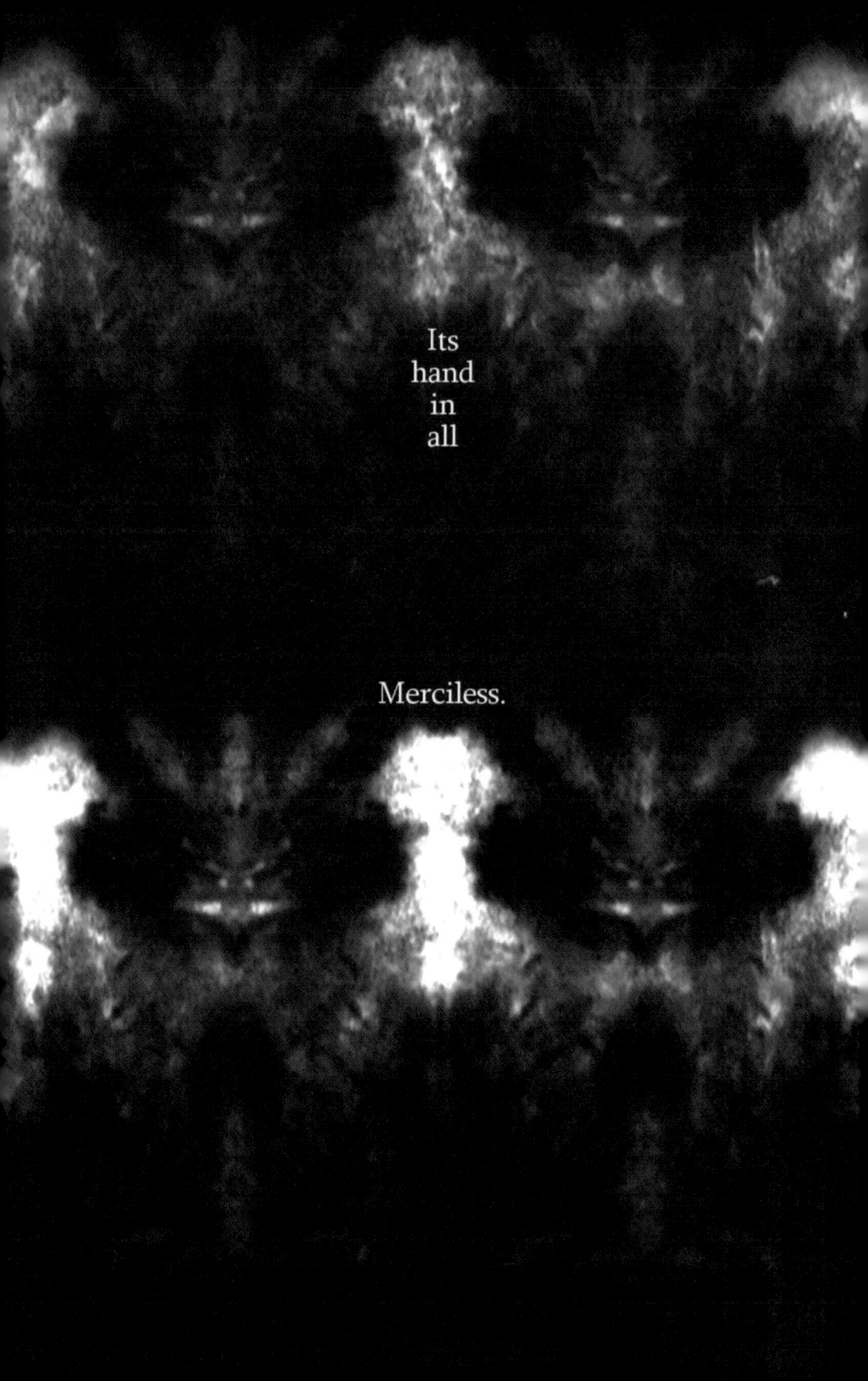

Its
hand
in
all

Merciless.

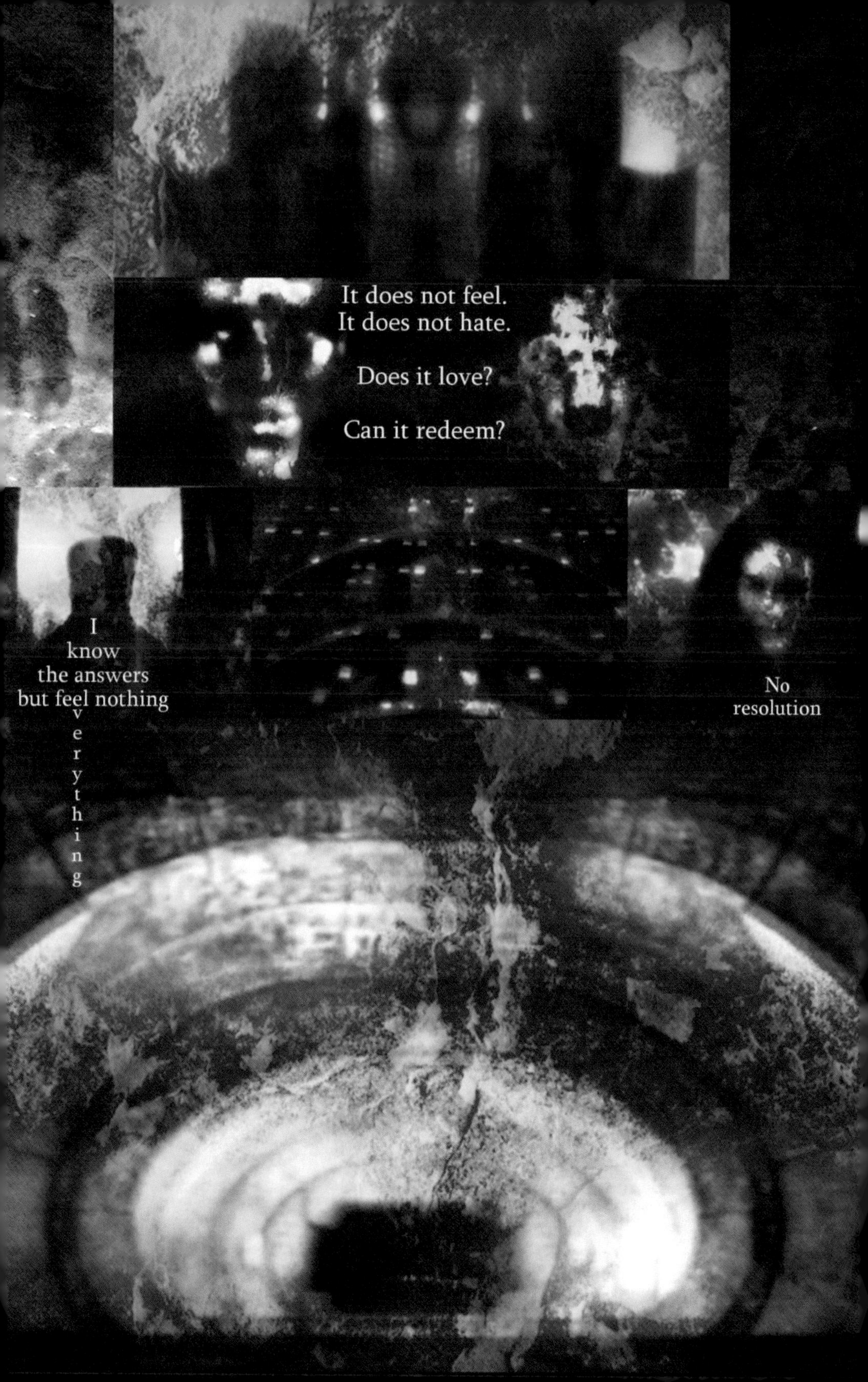
It does not feel.
It does not hate.
Does it love?
Can it redeem?
I know the answers but feel nothing
everything
No resolution

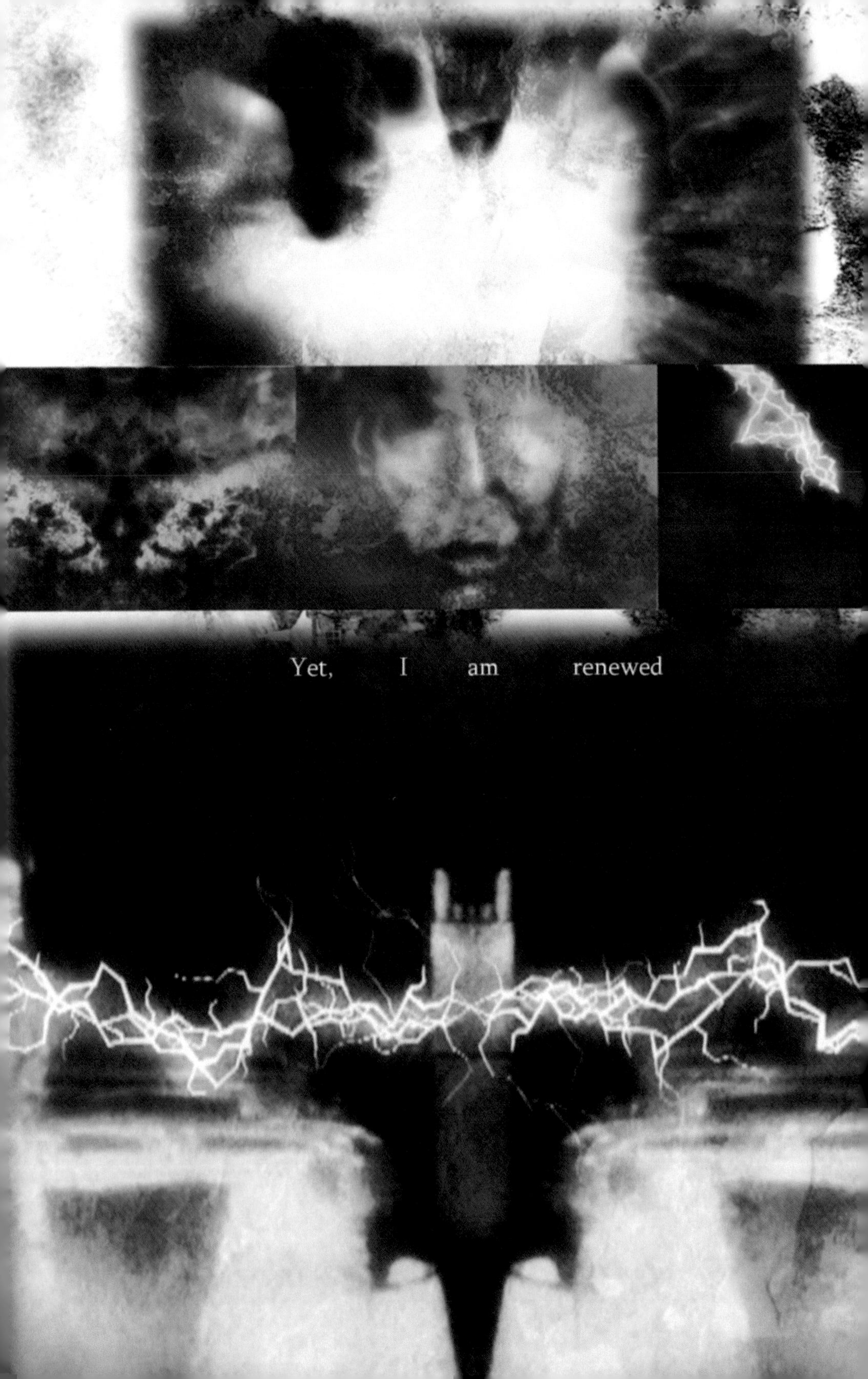
Yet, I am renewed

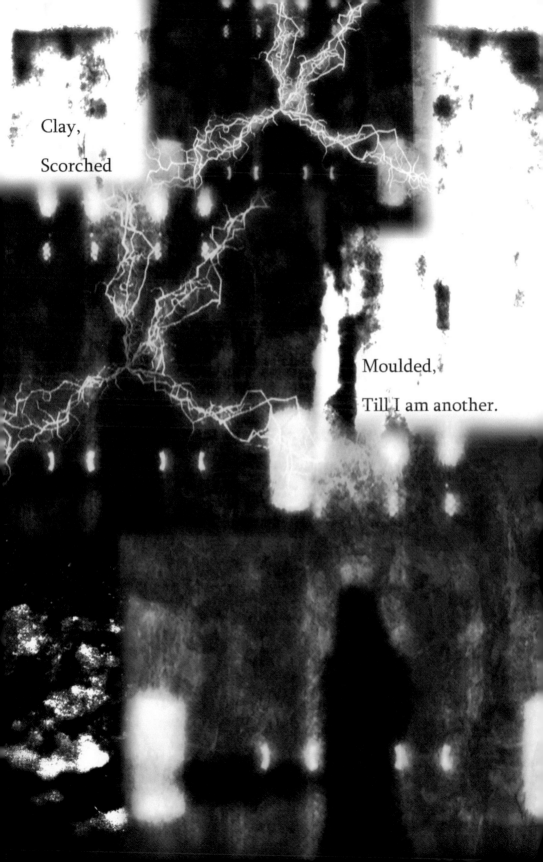

Clay,

Scorched

Moulded,

Till I am another.

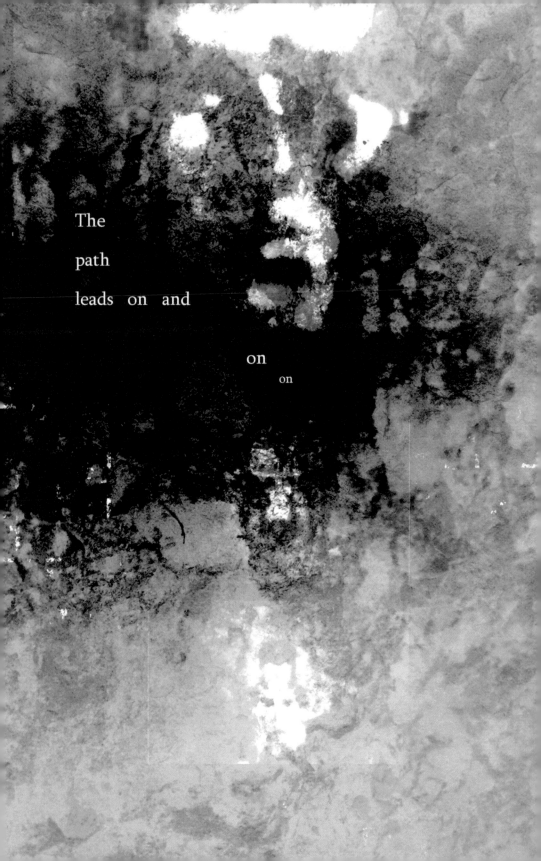

The

path

leads   on   and

on

on

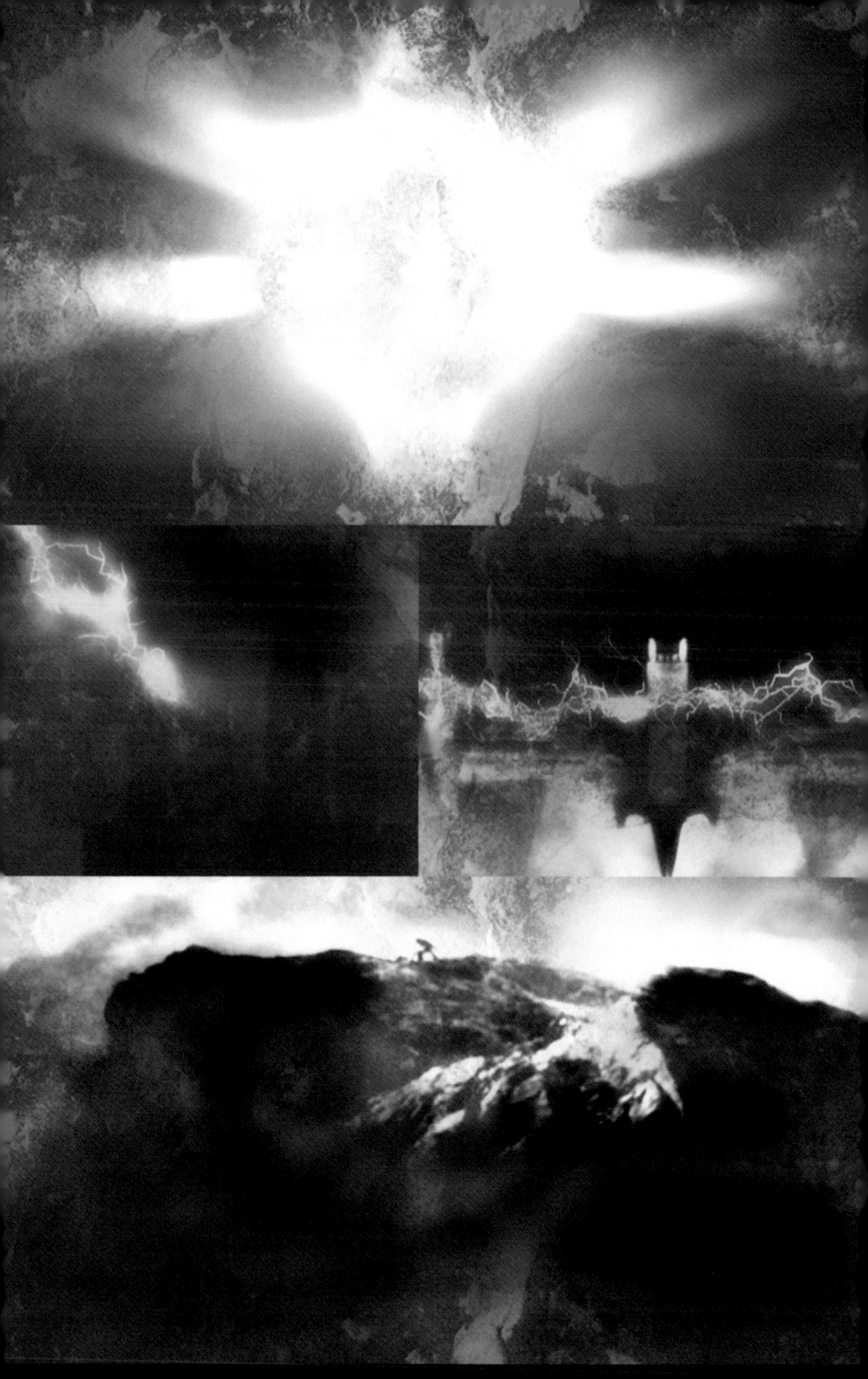

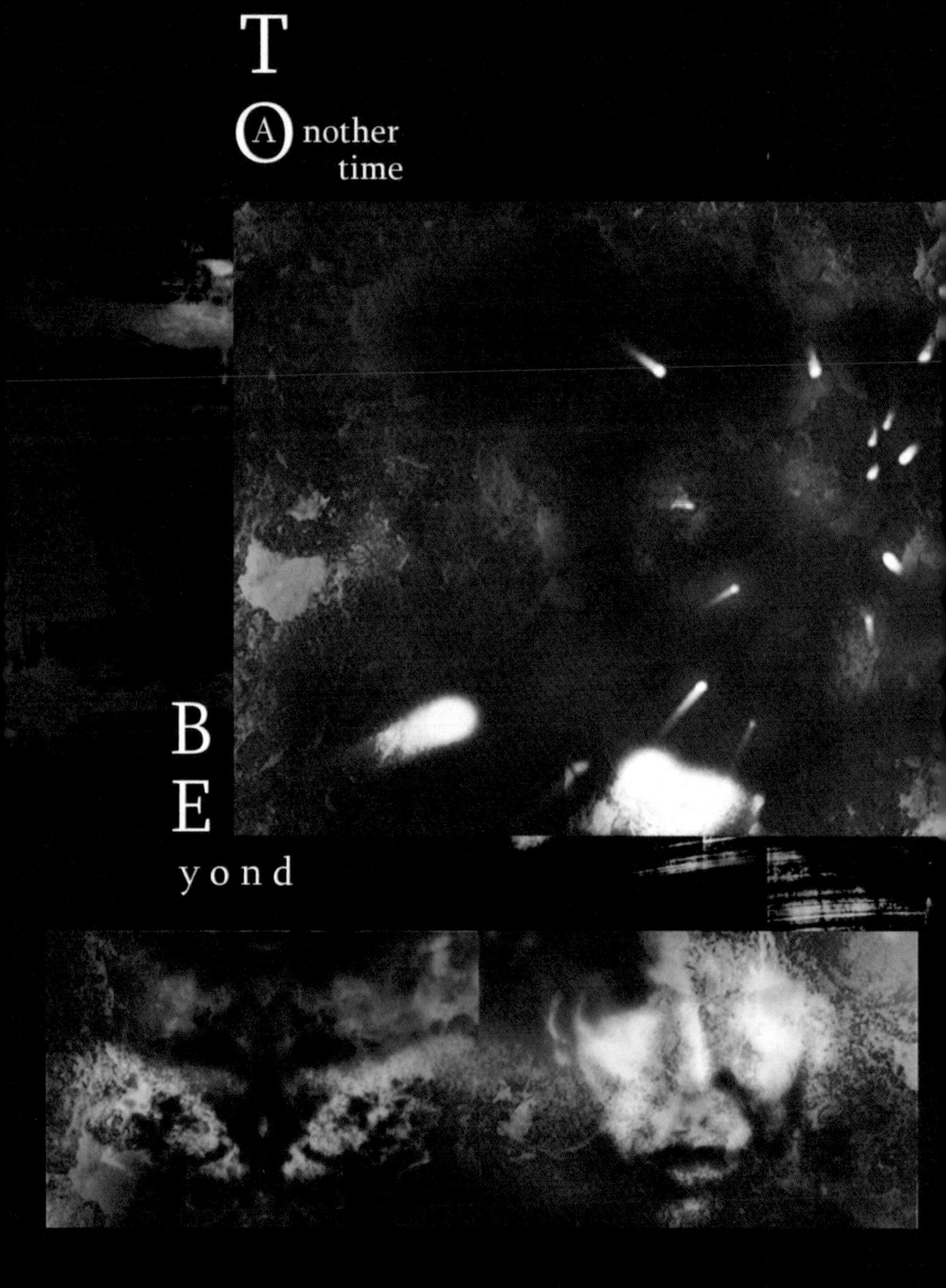
T
O Another time
BE
yond

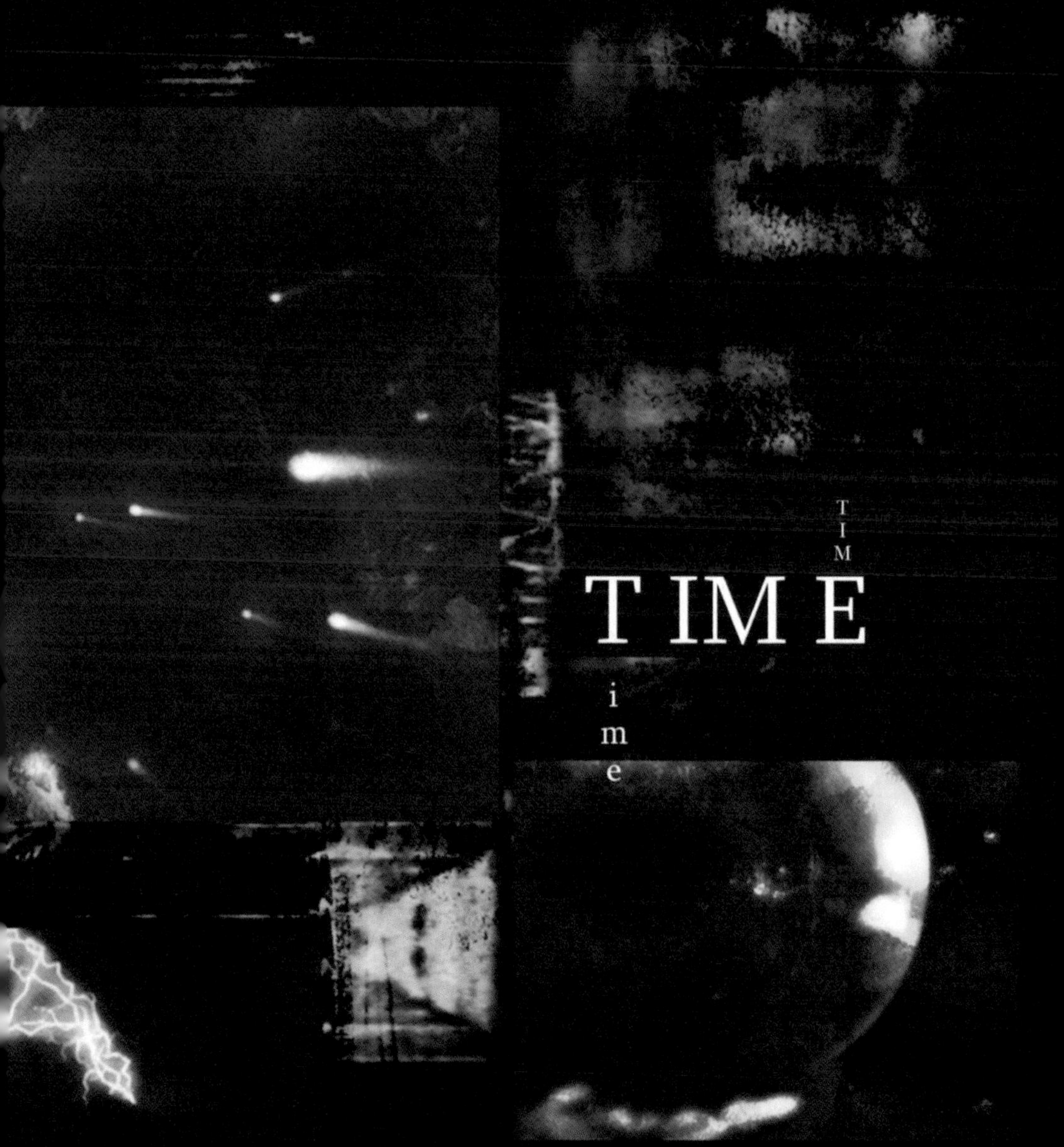
TIM
TIME
ime

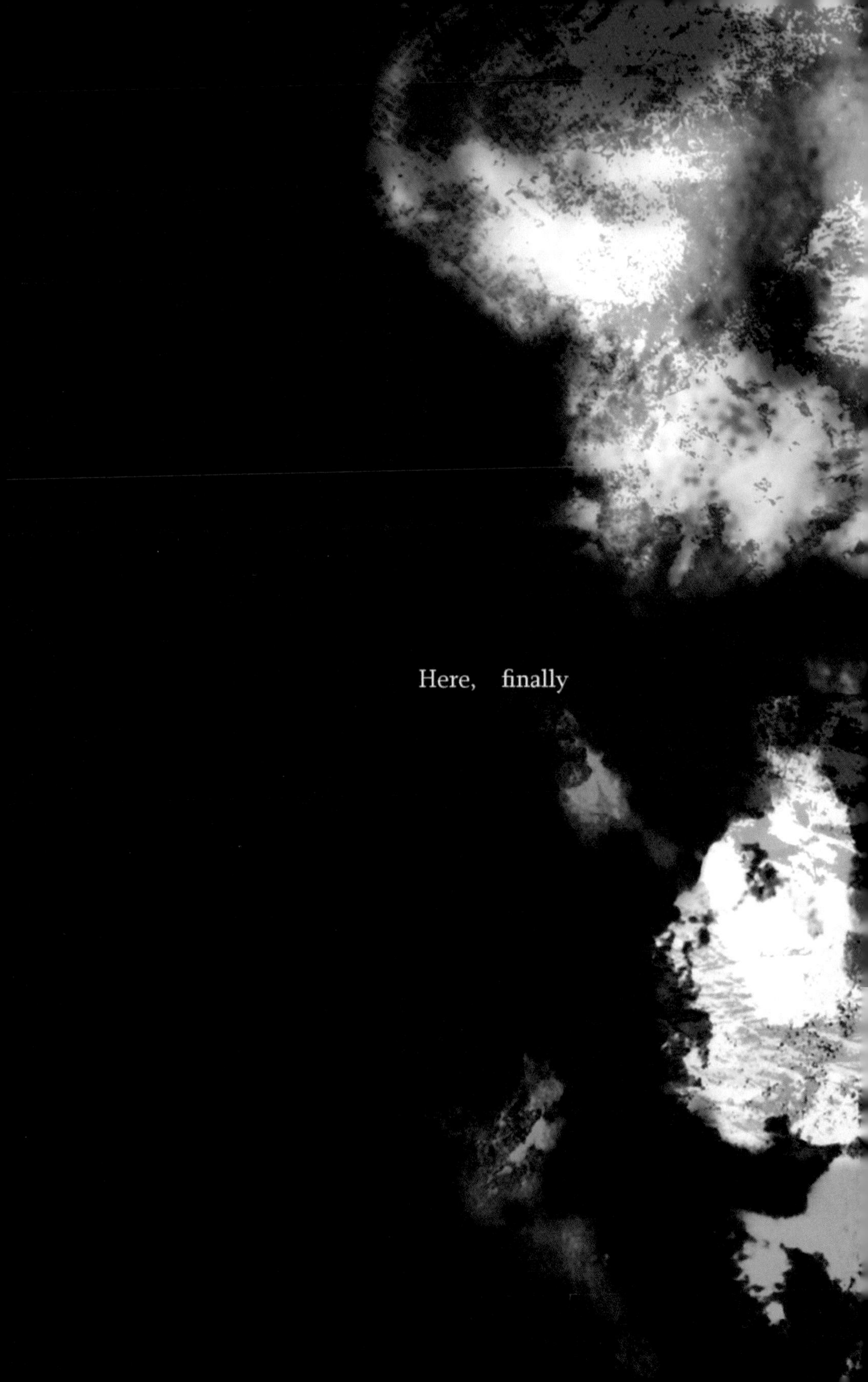

Here, finally

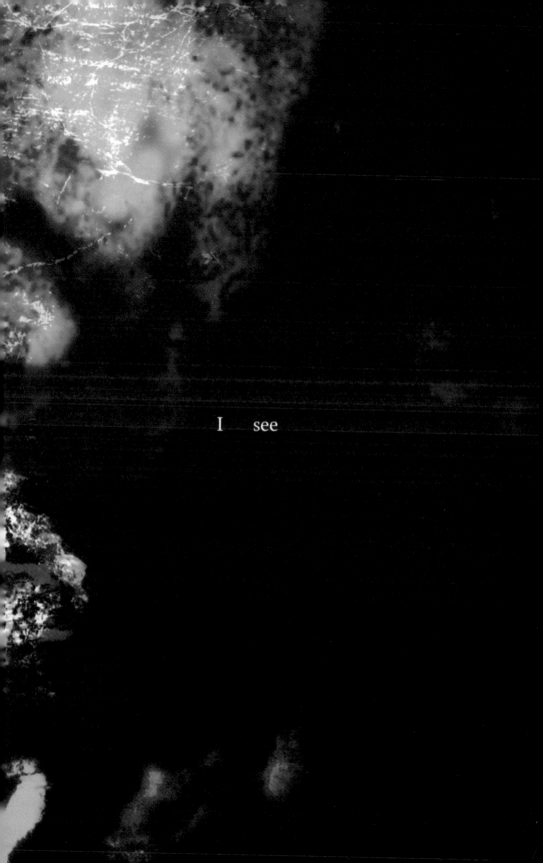

I   see

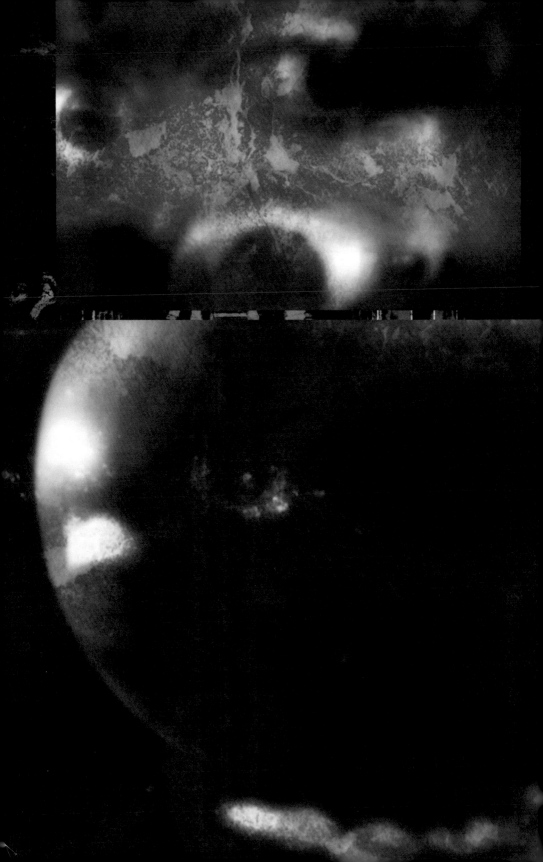

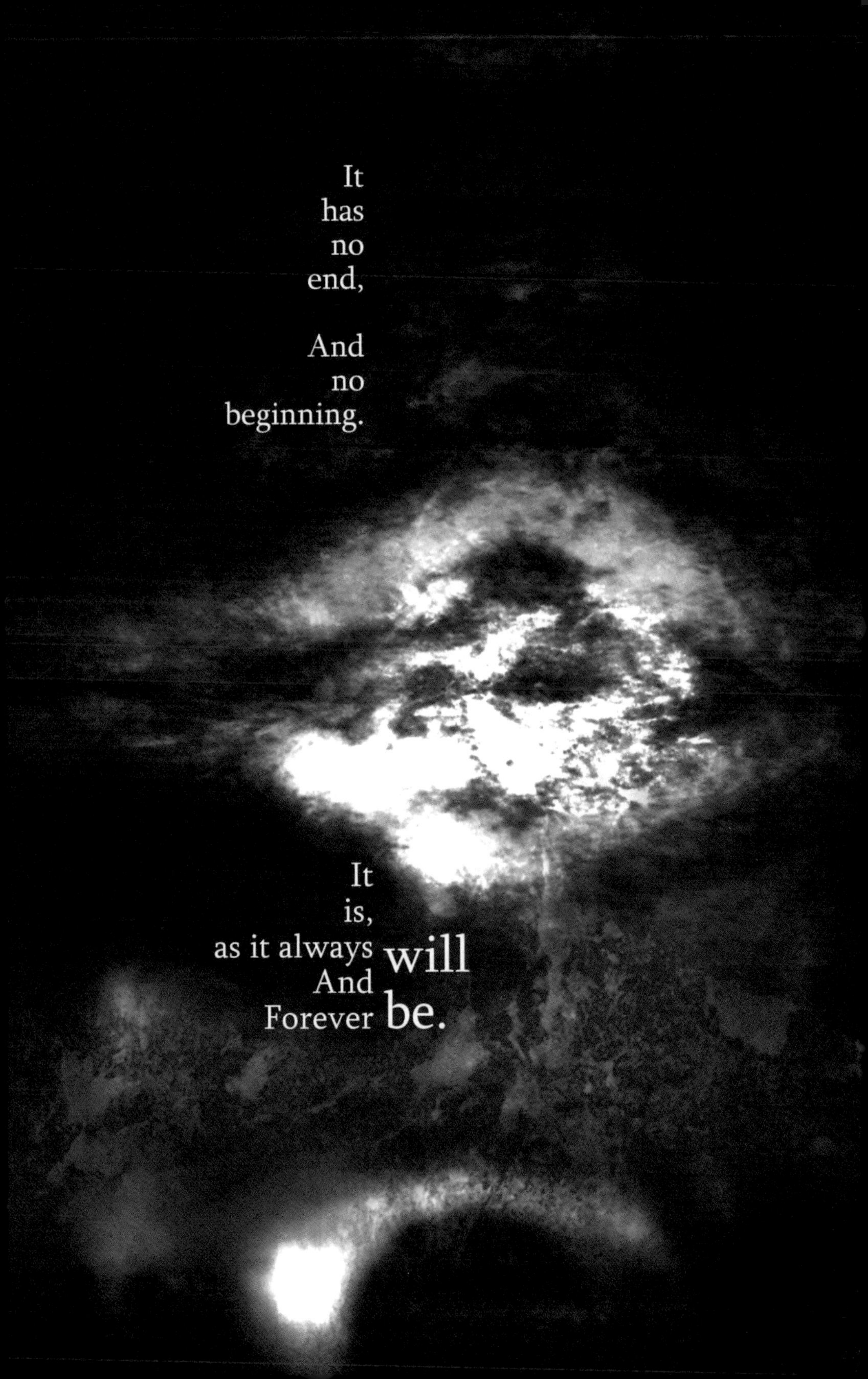

It
has
no
end,

And
no
beginning.

It
is,
as it always will
And
Forever be.

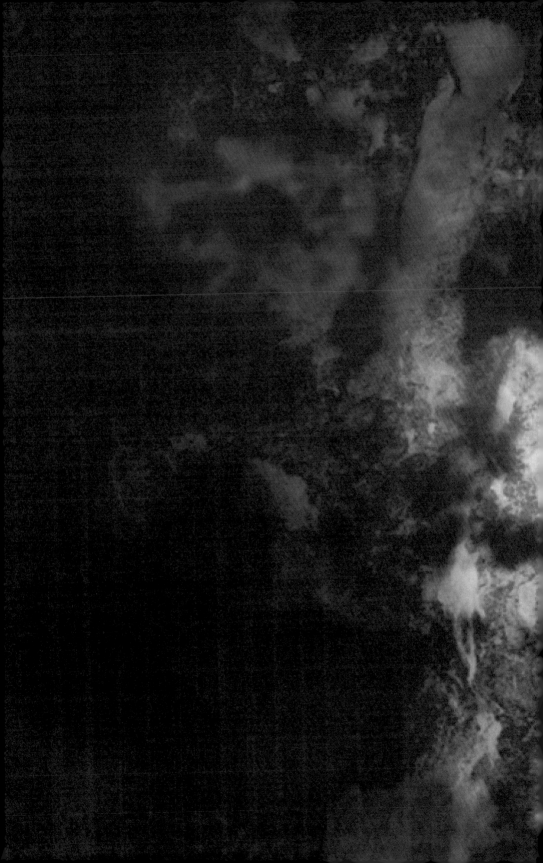

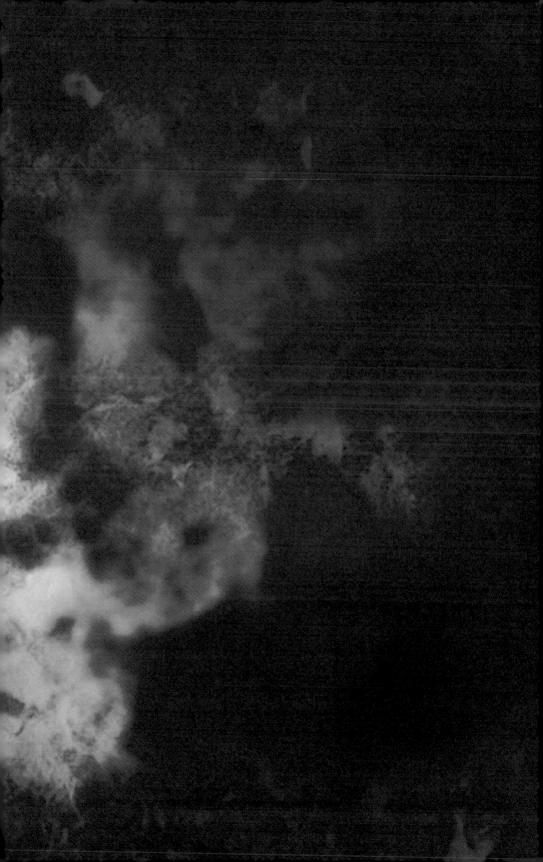

JOHN COCKSHAW

is a North Yorkshire-based artist and alumni of Sheffield Hallam University (BA Hons Fine Art and Mres in Art and Design 2002, 2003).

His principal interests as an artist are sequential photography and graphic art, landscape painting and work with a fantasy/sci-fi flavour. His Tolkien-inspired art has been exhibited at events in Oxford organised by The Tolkien Society, Sarehole Mill in Birmingham, with the Sociedad Tolkien Española in Seville, HobbitCon in Germany and more recently at NazgulCon in Sao Paolo, Brazil.

In December 2014, John curated an exhibition of international Tolkien-inspired artists at Curzon Ripon Arts/Cinema venue in North Yorkshire. Also a video artist, filmmaker and writer keen on developing his curatorial skills, John is most satisfied with multiple projects to work on.

ACKNOWLEDGMENTS

To Francesca T Barbini and Robert S. Malan for taking a leap of faith in collaborating on the *Sign of the Shining Beast* project.

ROBERT S MALAN

is a writer, hailing from Johannesburg, South Africa. Though he currently lives in Edinburgh, Scotland, Africa's unique and wonderful spirit remains indelibly etched on his psyche.

From an early age, he was drawn to studying a multitude of philosophies and belief systems, in particular Buddhism, Taoisim and Shamanism. He is especially fascinated by myth-legends, shaped in no small part by his interest in Old Testament tales, and the golden ages that shaped the Mayan, Egyptian and Cambodian temple complexes.

He is also a keen proponent and practitioner of Tai Chi, and other martial arts systems.

A Darkness in Mind: Quest & The Sign of the Shining Beast is his first published work. He is presently writing follow-up entries for the series in collaboration with John Cockshaw.

ACKNOWLEDGMENTS

Thanks to Jim Burns, Jay Johnstone, Ricardo Pinto and Ian Whates. Also to John Cockshaw - a kindred spirit, tireless in his excellent work. And too many friends to mention here, who have lent support and belief along the path.

Lightning Source UK Ltd.
Milton Keynes UK
UKIC03n0038030316
269494UK00003B/10

9 781911 143017